Welland Hendrick

A Brief History of the Empire State

Welland Hendrick

A Brief History of the Empire State

ISBN/EAN: 9783337169701

Printed in Europe, USA, Canada, Australia, Japan

Cover: Foto ©Andreas Hilbeck / pixelio.de

More available books at **www.hansebooks.com**

A

BRIEF HISTORY

OF THE

EMPIRE STATE

FOR

SCHOOLS AND FAMILIES

BY

WELLAND HENDRICK, A.M.

FOURTH EDITION, WITH REVISIONS

SYRACUSE, N. Y.

C. W. BARDEEN, PUBLISHER

1896

PREFACE.

When I began to teach American history in the schools of New York, I looked for a brief school history of the State. The book had to be written.

The study of the history of New York has a place in its schools :

1. The colony in its origin and growth was separate from the other colonies ; for fourteen years after the end of English dominion, the State was an independent nation ; and ever since, as a part of the American republic, it has had a distinct life.

2. Pupils commonly have a vague idea of the isolation of the original colonies and of the relation of the States under the confederation. During these periods a State history has a unity which a general history lacks. The best point of view for a beginner is the account of some one colony, in which he can trace the colony's earliest connection with neighboring provinces, its decreasing dependence upon the mother country, its consequent change from a colony to a State, and the reluctant but necessary giving up of State rights in the formation of a strong central government.

3. The study of State history is a study of civil government. It is a common experience that pupils, after taking up United States history, cannot distinguish between the duties of the State government and of the national government. It is the State which has to do with the every day life of the citizen ; and what a State is, is best learned in its history.

4. The importance of New York in the making of America has been underrated. The Minute Men, Faneuil Hall and the battle of Lexington are known ; but the Sons of Liberty, the Fields and

the battle of Oriskany are uncertain terms even to the people of
New York.   How the colony learned liberty under the Dutch, and
held to it through a century of English governors ; how the State,
fifth in number of people, with almost a third of its men tories,
with border open and chief city sure to be the enemy's headquarters, with much wealth in perishable shipping,—how such a State
was among the first in the war for freedom, and alone of the thirteen met every demand of congress ; how the commonwealth built
a canal which not only developed its interior, but also opened up
the great north-west ; how all these things were done, ought to be
taught with patriotic pride to the pupils of our public schools.

It has been my aim to prepare a brief history of New York suitable
for general reading, adapted to be a text-book for a short term's
work in the grammar or academic grades, and especially fitted for
a reader, either regular or supplementary, in any grade of work
after the fifth or sixth year.

It might be well for a class to read or study this book after it has
had a primary history of the United States, and before it takes
up the advanced study of that subject ; or the history of New York
may with profit be studied in connection with United States history.

In fact the history of New York properly taught is a history of
the United States ; and the teacher, who brings out in class the
facts here suggested but not detailed, can make the study a unified
and graphic story of the republic.

The book labors to be a consistent State history ; it does not
assume to give an account of national wars, presidential campaigns
and international affairs ; it refers to such topics only so far as they
throw light on the story of New York.   Men and affairs learned in
United States history may sometimes be found here in changed
relations : Hamilton, who devoted his genius to the nation, receives
less attention than DeWitt Clinton, who gave his life to the State.

Possibly the book lacks features that may be expected : it is not filled with praise of New York to the exclusion of all censure ; it does not insult the intelligence of the bright boys and girls of the junior grades by telling its story in baby-talk ; it does not relegate the gist of a page to fine-print notes at the bottom ; it does not crowd the account of the people, their customs and education, into the end of chapters, as if such matters were not indeed the truest part of all history.

While the book is not the result of original research, a wide range of authorities has been consulted, and the main facts selected and briefly put. Mention should be made in this connection of the history of New York by Ellis H. Roberts in the American commonwealth series, and of Mrs. Lamb's History of New York City.

W. H.

SARATOGA SPRINGS, N. Y., *August 21, 1890.*

A BRIEF HISTORY OF NEW YORK STATE.

CHAPTER I.

INTRODUCTORY.

Three men, Columbus. Cabot, and Hudson, introduce the history of New York State. One found the West Indies; another discovered the mainland and coasting southward may have seen the low-lying land of Long Island; while Henry Hudson, one hundred and seventeen years after the first voyage of Columbus, sailed into the bay of New York. It is possible that an Italian in the service of France, nearly a century before, found this bay and looked upon the river; it is certain that the Frenchman, Champlain, two months before the arrival of Hudson's Dutch crew, stood on the soil of the State; but the fame of Hudson is none the less. He may well be called the discoverer of New York ; he first made known to the world the advantages of the ample harbor,—the harbor that makes New York city the commercial capital of America.

The Land and the People.—But it is not upon this harbor alone that the importance of the State rests; its soil and its geographical position fit it for an empire. Within its boundaries the white man found the Iroquois, the conquering Indians of America. These red men were superior to other Indians; they lived in houses, had fields of corn, beans and tobacco, made earthenware, baskets and ropes, and the five tribes, Mohawks, Oneidas, Onondagas, Cayugas and Senecas were joined in a rude republic. These people were

(9)

known and feared all east of the Mississippi; but they chose a place for their corn fields and log houses in central New York, and near the present site of Syracuse they had their council-fire or capitol. From this advantageous centre they could go north by Lake Ontario and the St. Lawrence, east by the Mohawk, south to the Atlantic by the Susquehanna, south to the inland by the Allegany and Ohio, west by the great lakes. "New York," says Bancroft, "united richest lands with the highest adaptation to foreign and domestic commerce."

The Iroquois occupied the Mohawk valley and central and western New York, while they left the eastern and south-eastern parts to weaker Algonquin tribes, among whom were the Mohegans on the east bank of the Hudson and the Delawares along the river of that name. To the north and in Canada were other bands of Algonquins who long waged unsuccessful warfare with the Iroquois. These weaker Indians implored the help of the French; for French adventurers and traders had built forts along the St. Lawrence seventy years before Hudson's ship anchored off Sandy Hook.

Champlain, the "Father of New France," was finally persuaded by the neighboring friendly Indians to join in an expedition against the Iroquois. He went up the Sorel, found the lake to which he gave his name, and on its banks in Essex county met the Iroquois. Here on a July morning of 1609 the Indians of New York first saw the white man and heard the noise of his gun. They ran. For Champlain it was an easy victory; but it was a fatal blunder. Without knowing it

SAMUEL CHAMPLAIN.

he had made lasting enemies of the fiercest warriors of the continent. Again Champlain tried to penetrate the State from Lake Ontario, and getting as far as Madison county went back defeated. Again other Frenchmen tried to gain a foothold in New York State and failed because of the enmity of the Iroquois. Thus on the north the French were kept from New York while on the south the feeble colonies of the Dutch and English grew strong and held the land.

Periods.—The recorded history of New York, which begins with Champlain's battle on the shore of the lake, easily separates into five periods.

Period First.—The Rule of the Dutch,—extending from the discovery by Hudson in 1609 to the surrender to the English in 1664. In this period the Dutch discover and settle the land about the Hudson and on Long Island.

Period Second.—The Rule of the English,—extending from the surrender to the English in 1664 to the flight of the English governor in 1775. In this period the colonists increase rapidly; they drive back the French and find English rule unbearable.

Period Third.—New York as a Sovereign State,—extending from the flight of the English governor in 1775 to the inauguration of Washington in 1789. In this period the State joins with twelve other States in a war of independence, is one of a weak confederacy, and finally becomes part of a strong nation.

Period Fourth.—The Development of the State,—extending from the inauguration of Washington in 1789 to the completion of the Erie canal in 1825. In this period the State builds a waterway of national importance and advances from the rank of fifth to the rank of first in wealth and population.

Period Fifth.—The Era of Progress,—extending from the completion of the Erie canal in 1825 to the latter part of the nineteenth century. In this period the State maintains its right to the name of the Empire State.

PERIOD I.

CHAPTER II.

The Rule of the Dutch.—1609–1664.

Henry Hudson.—It was in July of 1609, as has been said, that Champlain first entered the State of New York. It was on the third of September of the same year that Hudson discovered New York bay. Henry Hudson was an Englishman who engaged in the service of some Amsterdam merchants and set out to find a northeast passage to India. The daring sailor left Holland in the little ship, the Half Moon, and tried to reach India by sailing north of

HUDSON'S SHIP.

(12)

Sweden. He was driven back by the ice, but, still unwilling to give up turned straight about to find a westerly way to Asia.

He touched first the shores of New Foundland, steered south, mended his sails in Maine, saw Chesapeake bay, and turning back to the north entered the river to which others have given his name. Knowing nothing of the breadth of the continent, he hoped that the stream would prove a passage to the Pacific; but when he had followed the river for over a hundred miles and found it growing shallow, he turned back; then having spent about a month inside Sandy Hook, he steered out into the deep, never again to return. On his next voyage, still looking for a north-west passage, he entered Hudson Bay. Here with his little son he was set adrift by his rebellious crew and perished.

The First Settlements.—Although the Cabots had discovered the continent more than a hundred years before the voyage of the Half Moon, yet the favored spot thus found by the Dutch was in the midst of a vast unclaimed wilderness. Hundreds of miles to the south were a few starving Englishmen at Jamestown; far to the north were camps of French traders among the snows of Nova Scotia and Montreal; all else was forest and savages. The May-flower had not sailed. When another or perhaps a second summer came around, the Indians, who had watched the sails of Hudson disappear, gladly welcomed the ships of some Dutch fur traders. These men bought and sold and went back.

Thus they continued going and coming, until in the fourth year after the discovery the traders built a few huts on Manhattan Island, so that it is said that New York was settled in 1613. Soon after, a strong building was put up where the foot of Broadway now is, to serve as a store-house and fort. About the same time the adventurous traders made their way nearer the heart of the fur trade and built a fort on Castle Island, below the present Albany.

But cabins, forts, and store-houses did not really make a settlement; they were shelters but not homes.

THE FIRST WAREHOUSE.

Discoveries and Claims.—While many of the thrifty Dutch were busy bartering their brass trinkets and fiery liquor for the skins of otters and beavers, other visitors to the new land were following the lead of Hudson and examining the coasts. Captain May sailed about Delaware Bay and left his name on its northern cape. Adrian Block, "first of European navigators steered through Hellgate" and sailed on Long Island Sound; he discovered the Connecticut river and found and named Rhode Island and Block Island.

From the discoveries of Hudson, Block and others the Dutch laid claim to the land and gave it a name. The Delaware they called the South river; the Connecticut the Fresh river; the Hudson the North river or the Mauritius (maw-rish-i-us). They called the country New Netherland, and claimed that it extended from the fortieth to the forty-fifth parallel of latitude. Later on they defined New Netherland as lying between the Delaware and Cape

Cod, and in later years they would have been glad to fix the Connecticut river as the northern and eastern boundary.

The First Homes.—These claims were held simply by trading posts until fifteen years after the discovery of Hudson, when thirty families of persecuted French protestants came. They were the first white people who made the land of New York their home. Eight of these families settled on the lower end of Manhattan island ; and about them grew the town called later New Amsterdam, destined to become New York city. Other families went to the New Jersey shore, where the land was called Pavonia. Eastward across the river from Manhattan on Long Island a little company of these people took the name Breukelen (Brooklyn). A few went to the Connecticut river and some to the Delaware

t' Fort nieuw Amſterdam op de Manhatans.

RUDE SKETCH OF NEW AMSTERDAM. (Made by a Dutch officer in 1635.)

river, while others sailed a short distance above the abandoned fort on Castle Island and built Fort Orange, the beginning of the city of Albany.

These families were sent out by a society of Dutch merchants called the Dutch West India company, an organization which had been chartered a few years before and which had received the entire control of New Netherland. The government of Holland still retained supreme authority over the territory; but all the internal affairs of the colony rested with the stockholders of the West India company.

The Patroons.—Beside sending these families, the company further encouraged settlements by the patroon system. They gave the right to any one who would establish a colony of fifty persons, to have and to hold forever a tract of land fronting sixteen miles on the water and running back indefinitely, provided however that the rights of the Indians were purchased. These large land owners were called patroons. One of the most famous of these patroons was Kilian Van Rensselaer (keé-le-än van ren'-sel-er) whose land, now in the counties of Albany, Columbia and Rensselaer, was known as Rensselaerwick. The patroons brought many people to New Netherland; but as they had almost boundless control over their settlements, they frequently quarreled with the West India company, with the colonists and with the governors.

The Goverment.—The first governor, or rather director-general, as he was called, was Peter Minuet, who was sent by the company and who began his rule in 1626. Two years before, Captain May had charge of the colony; but there was no formal government until the arrival of Minuet. He had a council of five to assist him and he appointed others to act as secretaries, sheriffs, collectors, and the like; but in the choice of none of these officers did the people have a part. Later on the colonists secured slight changes in the laws of the colony; but never did they obtain from Dutch rulers that the voice of the people should be heard in their own government.

During the thirty-eight years in which the Dutch had a formal government, four director-generals were in turn at the head of the colony: Peter Minuet, Walter Van Twiller, William Kieft (keeft), and Peter Stuyvesant (stī-ve-sant). The acts of these men were of little account; all of them did something for themselves and for the stockholders who sent them; none of them accomplished much for the people. Says some one rather severely: "Minuet was a self-willed and self-seeking adventurer, Van Twiller a drunken and indolent fool, Kieft a conceited and tyrannical bankrupt, Stuyvesant a despotic and passionate autocrat."

The first twelve years of authority was equally divided between Minuet and Van Twiller. The first governor was accused of favoring the patroons, and was recalled. Van Twiller, who has been made so laughable by Washington Irving, seemed to spend most of his small energy in personal quarrels. He wrangled with his officers, got into a dispute with the minister of the little church, and in turn was denounced from the pulpit. In his place William Kieft was sent. Where Van Twiller was slow and inefficient, Kieft was hasty and rash. To this rashness he added dishonesty, and in the ten years that he was director-general he brought the colony to the verge of ruin.

The Indians.—The greater part of Kieft's violent energy was spent upon the Indians. The decade in which he ruled was a time of Indian warfare. For the most part the colony had used the red men well and in return had received less trouble from them than had the neighboring settlements. The great industry of New Netherland was the fur trade; and for the success of this traffic peace with the Indians was necessary. So the Dutch were ever on good terms with the Iroquois, while the farmers and fishermen of New England were fighting King Philip, and the tobacco raisers of Virginia were suffering from the attacks of the tribe of Powhatan.

The Dutch made it a rule to buy the land which they occupied from the Indian owners. One of the first acts of Director Minuet was to purchase Manhattan Island for twenty-four dollars, at the rate of one cent for ten acres, paid in gay clothing, beads, and brass ornaments. So from the days of Henry Hudson for thirty years the savages did not trouble the colony. Soon after Kieft's arrival he found cause for dispute with the Raritan Indians on the New Jersey coast. He sent murdering expeditions, offered prizes for their heads, and caused Staten Island to become a slaughter ground.

PURCHASE OF MANHATTAN ISLAND.

The result of this was a gathering of the river Indians for the de-struction of the settlements. Still war could have been avoided by prudent means. It happened at this time that the Mohawks, of the Iroquois tribes, had bought for a round price in furs a few muskets, and were driving before them the Indians of the lower Hudson. The fugitives gathered around the Dutch settlements and asked for protection. Some of them camped at Pavonia; and while they were there a band of blood-thirsty colonists and soldiers easily got permission of Kieft, rowed across the river in a cold win-ter night, and before sunrise foully butchered eighty men, women, children, and babes. At Corlear's Hook, the foot of the modern Grand street, they murdered forty more. This was in 1643.

For two years the red men of Long Island and the Hudson val-ley, thus wantonly provoked and further incited by the brandy sold them, kept up a bloody contest. They drove the whites from the farms and villages until they forced them into Manhattan island. Outside of this retreat only Gravesend, Rensselaerwick, and Fort Orange were secure from attack. Many of the people returned to Holland; those who were left feared the Indians and detested Kieft; the settlements were in ruins and Manhattan could count but one hundred male citizens. Finally when a thousand Indians had been slain, and the very life of the colony was in danger, peace was made with the aid of the friendly Iroquois, and the colony began a new era of prosperity.

Growth of the Colony.—The settlements had increased, not rapidly, but sturdily. When Minuet came to be governor, New Netherland had a population of two hundred people. Twenty years later, at the close of Kieft's administration, this number had been increased ten-fold. These people,—no more than now are gathered in some of the small villages of the State,—lived on the lower end of Manhattan island; at Pavonia; at Brooklyn, which then stood a mile back from the river; at Fort Orange; at Fort

Good Hope, now Hartford; while farms spread over parts of the present counties of Albany, Rensselaer, Westchester, Richmond, Kings, and Queens. In the latter days of Dutch rule Esopus (e-so'-pus), now Kingston, was a brisk place on the Hudson; and Schenectady, first of the towns in the rich valley of the Mohawk, was begun. By this time it is estimated that the province had eight thousand inhabitants; while the future metropolis had a population of two thousand people.

The People of New Netherland.—These eight thousand people were by no means all from Holland. No other American settlement had so varied a class of inhabitants as had New York. "New York was always a city of the world." The colony by its offers of religious freedom attracted the persecuted from France, Germany, Bohemia, and all countries of Europe. And to the

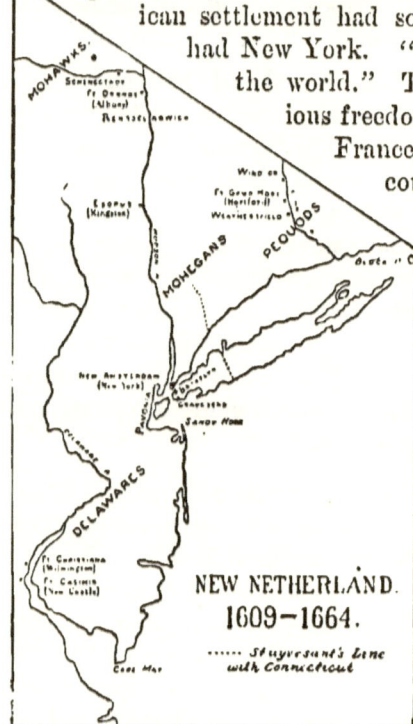

NEW NETHERLAND.
1609–1664.

...... Stuyvesant's Line
with Connecticut

shame of the colony it must be said that African slaves were of its population, brought in during the first year of Minuet's directorship, and afterwards greedily bought until the slave element became a source of danger. The most energetic part of the community came from the neighboring settlements of New England, some to seek superior soil, others to escape the persecution of the zealous Puritans. Among these were many Quakers and sturdy men most needed in the making of a state.

Stuyvesant.—Such citizens could not tamely submit to be misruled; they sent to Holland many bitter complaints, and welcomed with joy the recall of Kieft and the appointment of Peter Stuyvesant. This man, whose fame preceded him, was perhaps the best as he was the last of the Dutch governors. He had lost a leg in valiant service in the West Indies, and as he landed on a May day of 1647 at the port of New Amsterdam he stumped proudly along on his wooden leg, determined to conquer the huge difficulties which confronted him.*

The Swedes.—Four dangerous elements surrounded the new ruler,—the Swedes on the Delaware, the English on Long

Island and on the Connecticut river, the Indians, and the rapidly growing party in New Amsterdam who wanted a voice in making the laws and the rulers. The Swedes early claimed the attention of Stuyvesant. About the time that Kieft became director, a party from Sweden, led by Peter Minuet, smarting under his dismissal from the directorship, settled on the south bank of Delaware bay. Here on land claimed to belong to New Netherland they built Fort Christiana (kris-te-ah´-na), on the site of Wilmington, defied Kieft, and captured the Dutch fort, Casimir. They gave up however both strongholds to Stuyvesant on his arrival in the bay with a fleet and six hundred men; so that land now in the state of Delaware was for a time under the government at New York city.

STUYVESANT'S SEAL.

Further Indian Troubles.—While Stuyvesant was attending to these matters on the Delaware, the Indians took the opportunity

---

* His portrait faces the title-page of this volume.

to raid Hoboken and Pavonia; they killed a hundred settlers, and threatened another general outbreak. The governor on his return checked the slaughter, and by his prudent efforts to defend the colony rather than to kill off the Indians soon secured lasting peace; so never again was Manhattan in fear of savage war.

The English.—When the governor turned his attention toward the English on the Connecticut he found thrifty colonies. In the days of Van Twiller the Dutch had bought of the Pequod Indians a tract of land where Hartford now stands, and had there built Fort Good Hope. A few weeks later some people from Massachusetts sailed up the river, defied the guns of the little fort, and settled Windsor. Soon the Dutch fort was surrounded by the farms of the energetic Puritans. Van Twiller sent a company of seventy men to take an English fort at Weathersfield; they started with much noise of drum and with boasting; they came back without making an attack.

These Dutch on the eastern outpost of New Netherland were traders and soldiers; they grew discontented and died off. Their English neighbors were farmers: they took large harvests from the soil, brought up increasing families, and were content. They filled eastern Long Island; they crept into Westchester; they were likely to occupy the upper valley of the Hudson, cut off the fur trade of the Dutch, and hem them in on a narrow strip. When Stuyvesant took the colony in hand he saw that the best that he could do was to agree on a favorable boundary and give up all claim to the valley of the Connecticut. He conceded to the English all of Long Island that is now Suffolk county, running the dividing line south from Oyster Bay, and gained a promise that on the main land the Connecticut boundary should not come within ten miles of the Hudson river.

This treaty was never ratified by the English government; it was not respected by the colonists who made it. On Long Island they over-stepped the dividing lines. Stuyvesant sailed around to Boston to protest ; but he only showed his weakness. "Connecticut," said her agents at another time, "by its charter extends to the Pacific."—"Where then is New Netherland ?" asked the Dutch envoys.—"That," said the English coolly, "we do not know."

Dissatisfaction of the People.—But the danger fatal to Dutch interests was neither the Swedes, the Indians, nor the English. The very people of the colony oppressed by the greed of the West India company chafed under the control of Holland. There were high taxes on things bought and sold, on produce sent abroad, on goods received. In return the company promised to build defences and take the care necessary for settlements in a wilderness. It failed to do so ; the company itself did not prosper, but became bankrupt, and left the people without suitable protection from Indians and rival colonists.

There was no public spirit, for no one had a voice in the laws. Wealth could purchase certain privileges, but manhood had no rights. The settlers looked to their neighbors, the New England colonists, and saw more prosperous communities making their own laws in town meeting, and providing promptly for their defence. The comparison of the two provinces was surely not to the credit of the Dutch. Nor were there wanting plenty of English in New Netherland to call the attention of the Dutch to these facts. The English became so numerous that an English secretary, English preachers, and the writing of the laws in English became necessary. During the Indian war John Underhill, a former resident of Connecticut, who had gained fame in the Pequod war, was put at the head of the Dutch troops. The keen Yankees daily increased and thrived among the Dutch; they became their merchants, taught their schools, married their daughters, gave them their first lesson in resistance to tyrants.

The People Recognized.—Director Kieft had seen during the troublesome days of his rule that he must make a pretense of asking the wishes of the common people. So as a matter of policy he requested the patroons and heads of families to select a committee of twelve to advise together for the welfare of the colony. These twelve men were the first representative body of the people of the State of New York. Afterward there was a committee of a smaller number known as the eight men. As long as these committees favored higher taxes and Kieft's plans against the Indians, he willingly heeded them; when they opposed his schemes and demanded just laws for the inhabitants of the province, he sent them home.

His successor, Stuyvesant, allowed the towns of New Amsterdam, Brooklyn, Gravesend, and Amersfoort (Flatlands), to elect eighteen delegates, from whom he chose nine men to act as magistrates and as a body of advisers. But neither he nor the company would give them any real power. He answered the respectful appeals of the people: "Laws will be made by the director and council. Shall the people elect their own officers? Every man will vote for one of his own stamp. The thief will vote for the thief, and fraud and vice will become privileged!" He was praised by the company. "Have no regard to the consent of the people," said they; "let them indulge no longer the visionary dream that taxes can be imposed only with their consent."

The Surrender.—But the people continued to dream. The assembly was dismissed. Yet again in 1663 the stubborn governor was forced to allow another assembly from the villages to be called. Troubles were coming fast: Esopus was burned by the Indians; Long Island towns were revolting; at Gravesend, almost within sight of New Amsterdam, the Dutch flag was torn down and the English colors shown; the Connecticut Yankees had bought of the Indians land up to the Hudson: rumors of the coming of an English fleet were in the air. The rumors had truth in them.

Late in August of the year 1664, a fleet with English soldiers and with men of Massachusetts and Connecticut anchored in Gravesend Bay. The defences of the city were weak; many of the people were willing to try English rule ; the burgomasters advised surrender. " I would rather be carried to my grave," said the unconquerable Stuyvesant. But without death or wound, on the third of September, fifty-five years to a day from Hudson's discovery, the people of New Netherland took the authority into their own hands, agreed to deliver it to the English, and brought the rule of Stuyvesant to an end.

His bravery earned a better fate. As the hired agent of the West India Company he did as they directed. His ideas of human liberty were too narrow to allow him to see that his duty to his employers was at enmity with a higher duty to the people. But he had the good of the colony at heart. With the settlers he quietly spent his after life, and among the busy streets of the great city, which once as a village he governed, is his grave.

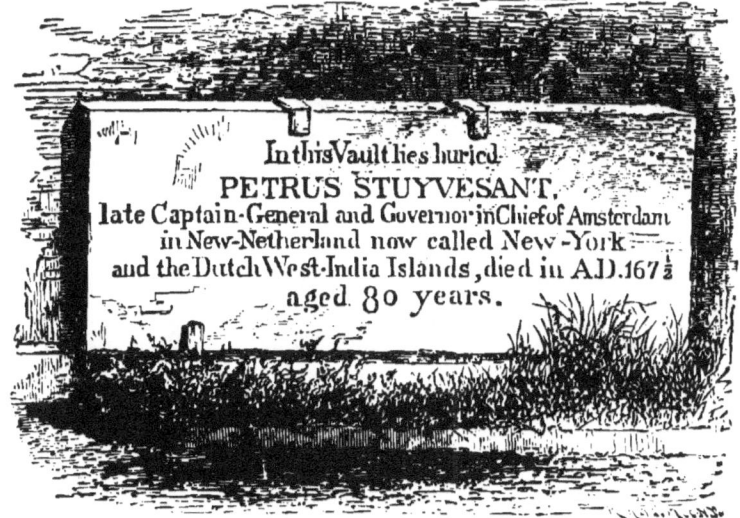

In this Vault lies buried
PETRUS STUYVESANT.
late Captain-General and Governor in Chief of Amsterdam
in New-Netherland now called New -York
and the Dutch West-India Islands, died in A.D. 167½
aged 80 years.

STUYVESANT'S TOMB.—(St. Mark's Church, New York City.)

CHAPTER III.

Why the Dutch Lost New York.—Holland did not lose New Netherland because inferior as a nation to England. The Dutch Republic during the first half of the seventeenth century was one of the great powers of Europe; she had gained her independence from the tyranny of Spain; her capital, Amsterdam, was the commercial centre of the world; her victorious admiral, Von Tromp (Trömp) swept the seas with a broom at his mast head; her schools, writers and statesmen were among the most famous of Europe.

Nor did the Dutch lose their colony because their title to the land was less valid than that of England. They based their claim first on the discovery of Hudson, secondly on actual settlement, thirdly on purchase of the land from the Indians. The sole title of the English to the soil lay in the coasting voyages of the Cabots from New Foundland to Maryland over a hundred and fifty years before. The rights of the Indians they counted as nothing.

The Dutch lost New York because as traders and soldiers they could not hold the land against the English farmer. The contest for the Connecticut valley was the critical event. To a great extent the Dutch farmers along the Hudson rented their land of the patroons and hence were not attached to the soil as were the New England settlers who owned the land which they plowed. The Dutch Republic blundered when it gave New Netherland into the hands of a money-getting company; the West India company blundered when it gave its best lands to the king-like patroons.

(26)

Leading Men.—During the fifty years of Dutch control the simple affairs of the small band of colonists called forth few men worthy to be remembered. Of the governors Stuyvesant was the only one of ordinary ability. Among the patroons was David Pietersen de Vries (pee-ter-sen deh vrees) who defended the interests of the people; he had the courage to censure Van Twiller for his inefficiency and to oppose the fool-hardy projects of Kieft. He was president of the Twelve, that germ of a government of the people. Finally having been ruined by the Indian war he went back to Holland. When parting with Kieft he said, "The murders in which you have shed so much innocent blood will yet be avenged on your own head;" a prophecy soon fulfilled by the shipwreck of the governor when recalled to Holland.

Another leader of the people was Dominie John Megapolensis, who came as a minister to Rensselaerwick. He carried the gospel to the Indians, who had already heard something of the story of the cross from the French priests of Canada. Later the good Magapolensis lived on western Long Island and always appeared as the champion of the people.

The one man who without rank or wealth rose from among the ordinary colonists to make his mark in history was Arendt Van Curler. He was the first white man from the Dutch settlements to penetrate the Mohawk valley. He reported the lands "the most beautiful that eye ever saw." Van Curler or Corlear as the Indians called him secured the love and trust of the Iroquois to a wonderful degree. To them he was the greatest of white men and ever afterward they called the governor of New York " Brother Corlear." During the last years of Dutch rule he pushed out from Fort Orange with a company of colonists and settled Schenectady, long the outpost of the great west,

The Common People.—Though the colony produced few men of note, the general character of the people was of a high order; they were thrifty, neat and industrious. "They brought over with them the liberal ideas and homely virtues and honest maxims of their country." There were few that were lazy, and no paupers. They had little mercy for criminals; a man for stealing some "nose-cloths" was banished; a slanderer had a red hot iron stuck through his tongue. Women were forbidden to scold; and for that and like offences there was a ducking stool on Manhattan island near the water's edge. Just in front of the fort was a gallows, one of the first objects to be seen by the new-comer sailing up the bay to New Amsterdam.

New Amsterdam.—That settlement had been incorporated as a separate village in 1653, when it had less than a thousand people. It was some years before the first street was paved with stone; and there was much trouble because the "broad-way" leading from the fort was rooted up by hogs. Thereupon a city ordinance was made, hardly necessary in modern New York, compelling the owners to stick rings through the hogs' noses. All over the new city the gardens and yards were luxurious with cabbages and tulips. The

VIEW OF NEW AMSTERDAM IN 1656.

homes, first of logs, soon came to be like the odd looking, comfortable dwellings of the mother country.

Houses.—The Dutch house, still to be seen in old towns about the Hudson, stood gable end to the street. The front wall was generally of brick or stone, while the rest of the house was wooden, and instead of slanting to a point, like the tiled roof, the wall went up to a peak in steps like a pair of stairs. Scattered about on the

DUTCH HOUSES IN NEW AMSTERDAM.

front of the house were large iron figures which told the date of the building. Deep-seated windows with small panes of glass looked upon the street, and on a dark night contained a lighted candle; while the lighting of New Amsterdam's streets was further secured by requiring every seventh householder to "hang out a lanthorn and candle on a pole." Within were broad halls, sanded floors, large rooms in front, where the good vrow gave weekly vent to her passion for cleaning house, and small rooms in the rear where the family lived. The furniture was ponderous, the articles of cooking were quaint and ungainly to modern eyes, and the huge Dutch oven was the pride of the house.

Stadthuys.
(STATEHOUSE.)

Daily Life.—If we are to gather our ideas of the early Dutch settlers from Washington Irving's Knickerbocker's History of New York, the founders of the metropolis ate breakfast at sunrise, dined at eleven, and at sunset went to bed. They ate potatoes, cabbages, asparagus, and barley bread; had plenty of game and poultry for their table; delighted in clams, calling them clippers, and in doughnuts, calling them olykocks; drank much buttermilk and tea, and smoked immoderately.

Dress.—The hair of the women was "pomatumed back from their foreheads with a candle and covered with a cap of quilted calico." "Their petticoats of linsey-woolsey were striped with a variety of gorgeous dyes" and "scarce reached below the knee." Mynheer (min-hēr) wore about his ample form a linsey-wolsey coat, the work of his good vrow (frow), as was most of the clothing of the family. A hat very low in the crown and very broad in the brim sat upon his head ; large brass buttons decked his coat and immense shining buckles set off his shoes ; while his many pairs of galligaskins or breeches were drawn on one above another until they rendered him still more portly than nature intended.

Religion.—Good natured as their habits show them to be, the early Dutch of New York were likewise liberal in their views of religious liberty. New Netherland gave a hearty welcome to peaceable comers of every religious belief with the same spirit in which Holland harbored the Puritans from England. The colony did not reach the high standard of perfect religious liberty, first known in Rhode Island ; but it stood far in advance of the narrow policy of Massachusetts and Virginia.

There was a recognized religion of the government, that of the Dutch Reformed church ; and Stuyvesant, who carried his military spirit into religion as well as into politics, tried to drive out a rival body, the Lutheran church ; but he was rebuked by the West India company, and saw the persecuted sect flourish. A few Quakers were banished but for the most part, they were gladly received. Catholics, Protestants, and Jews worshipped as they liked ; and in the latter days of Dutch dominion there were said to be fourteen organized denominations in the province, more indeed than there were ministers.

The first minister, Everardus Bogardus, came with Van Twiller. The salary of one of his brother ministers has been left on record as being one hundred and fifty beaver skins, lawful coin of the realm. The minister of New Netherland, or "dominie" as he was called, while he was not the important officer that he was in the austere Puritan settlements, was held by the jolly burghers in high esteem.

Education.—In the same ship with Dominie Bogardus came the pioneer school-master of New York State, Adam Roelandsen. Probably as the most of his calling did in those days, he added to his income by digging graves, ringing the church bell and leading the choir. The patroon act required a school teacher to be placed on each of the estates ; and in general the state papers of the colony recognized the importance of education. But evidently the practice of the money-getting settlers did not keep pace with their theories. Still they took care that a school teacher should be found in every village ; and in one case the tuition was announced as two beaver skins a year. In Stuyvesant's time a Latin school of some fame was established at New Amsterdam.

The Result of Dutch Customs can still be easily traced

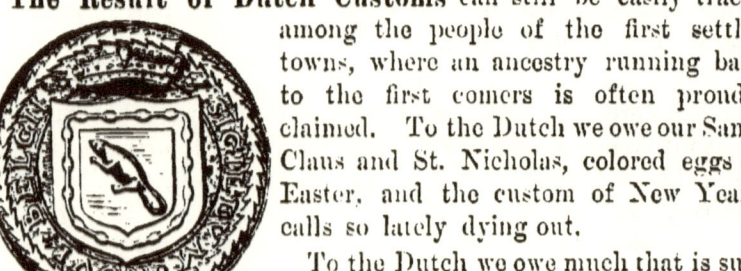

among the people of the first settled towns, where an ancestry running back to the first comers is often proudly claimed. To the Dutch we owe our Santa Claus and St. Nicholas, colored eggs at Easter, and the custom of New Year's calls so lately dying out.

To the Dutch we owe much that is substantial in the growth of the State; though

SEAL OF NEW NETHERLAND, 1623. often amid change and rapid progress we have lost sight of the source. To the Dutch we certainly owe above all else the principles of commercial integrity and of far-sighted business policy, which, brought from the old Amsterdam to the new, became the foundation of the greatness of New York State.

SUMMARY OF EVENTS,—PERIOD FIRST.

1497-98. Probable voyage of the Cabots past Long Island coast.
1524.   Doubtful discovery of New York bay by Verrazani.
1609.   Hudson's discovery.
          Discovery of Lake Champlain.
1613.   Building of traders' huts on Manhattan island.
1614.   Building of Fort Nassau on Castle island.
          Block's discovery of the Connecticut.
1615.   Champlain's second expedition into New York.
1621.   The Dutch West India company chartered.
1623.   Arrival of the first families in New Netherland.
1624.   May director.
1625.   Verhulst director.
          Brooklyn settled.
1626.   Minuet director-general.
          Manhattan island bought of the Indians.
1629.   Privileges granted to patroons.
1633.   Van Twiller director-general.
          Fort Good Hope built on the Connecticut.
1638.   Kieft director-general.
          Arrival of the Swedes in Delaware.
1640.   War with the Raritan Indians.
1641.   Appointment of the twelve men as representatives.
1643.   Murder of the Indians at Pavonia.
          General Indian outbreak.
1645.   Peace made by the settlers and Iroquois with the river
            tribes.
1647.   Stuyvesant director-general.
1653.   An assembly of the villages called.
1655.   Dutch conquest of New Sweden.
          Indian outbreak around Manhattan island.
1661.   Schenectady founded by Arendt Van Curler.
1664.   Surrender to the English.

PERIOD II.

CHAPTER IV.

NEW YORK UNDER THE DUKE OF YORK.—1664-1688.

About the time of the discovery of New York, a company of English Puritans, persecuted for their religion, fled to Holland. They asked the Dutch authorities to be allowed to settle in the new country. They were refused and sailing for English soil landed, as the world knows, at Plymouth Rock, on the twenty-first of December, 1620. This was three years before the arrival of the first families in New Netherland. Had the Puritans' request been granted, the entire history of America would have been changed.

The Duke of York.—These men of New England by emigrating to New Netherland helped to accomplish, what the Dutch authorities had at first feared, the capture of the province by the British crown. Meanwhile in England the Puritans had driven out the king and placed Oliver Cromwell at the head of the government. Soon after Cromwell's death, however, Charles II. returned to the throne, in 1660; and one of his first acts was to give to his brother, James, Duke of York, all the land lying between the Connecticut and Delaware rivers. The Duke to secure this gift, which was not his brother's to give, armed and sent out a fleet under the command of Colonel Richard Nichols. The easy conquest of Nichols was a deed of robbery. There was not even the excuse of war, since Holland and England were at peace. So that it is little to the credit of the conquerors that they offered the surprised garrison favorable terms and encouraged the Dutch settlers to remain on their lands.

(34)

The Beginning of English Rule.—The eight or nine thousand colonists now found themselves in a province named New York, in honor of the Duke. New York was the name given to New Amsterdam also, and as if that was not enough, the fort was called Fort James and Fort Orange was called Albany from another title of the Duke. The director-general became governor; the burgomasters, magistrates; the schepens, aldermen; the schouts, sheriffs; the koopmen, secretaries. But the change in the affairs of the colony was mostly a change of name. True, the people received assurance of religious liberty, equal taxation, toleration of former customs and the security of land titles; but they obtained nothing of the coveted New England liberty, no right to elect their officers and to levy the taxes.

The First English Governor, to whom all this power was given, was Colonel Nichols himself. The most important of his appointments was that of Thomas Willet to be the first mayor of New York city,—a city which was then incorporated after the manner of English towns. Nichols had received from the Duke on leaving England minute orders for the government of the colony which he was expected to seize. These instructions placed in his hands more power than the governor of any other English colony in America had,—more power than even the Dutch governors had possessed. In many respects Nichols was no more able ruler than were the Dutch director-generals; but he had one quality which they had not—the tact to manage the people.

He needed all his ingenuity, for he had to control a people two-thirds of whom had customs and a language different from his own; and he had to levy heavy taxes in order to prepare the forts for the expected attempt of Holland to regain the stolen colony. He succeeded in making himself more popular with the Dutch than with the English. The Puritan inhabitants of Long Island and Westchester, a part of the colony then known as Yorkshire, had been brought up to believe in the town meetings of New England; and at an assembly called to meet at Hempstead, thirty-four delegates appeared and asked for the right to elect their officers. This they were refused by the governor, and, having nothing else to do, obediently agreed to a code of laws made out by the Duke and known as "The Duke's Laws."

Neighboring Colonies.—The grant to the Duke of York was, as has been said, of the land between the Connecticut and the Delaware; and the same paper gave him a claim to all of the islands between Cape Cod and Cape May. Connecticut, however, had no more intention of giving her settlements on eastern Long Island and on the west bank of the Connecticut river to an English colony than to the Dutch; but rather than quarrel with Nichols, her people agreed to leave the disputed boundary to a commission. The men thus appointed gave to New York all of Long Island, much to the disgust of its eastern towns, and to Connecticut a favorable boundary on the main land, about indeed as it now remains.

When Governor Nichols saw such a considerable portion taken from the eastern side of his province, he turned to the western boundary, and found there a still larger part gone; for the Duke, unknown to Nichols, had given to Lord Berkeley and Sir George Carteret the land lying between the Hudson and the Delaware. To this caprice of the Duke is due the fact that there is a State of New Jersey, and that New York is not bounded on the south by Delaware bay. For some years still the present State of Delaware was a part of New York until bought by William Penn; and for a long time tribute was exacted from Nantucket and Martha's Vineyard.

Change of Governor; Condition of the Colony.—What was left of the Duke's grant was quite enough to worry the well-meaning Nichols. The work was hard, the honor and pay small; and he obtained his recall. A little later while fighting the **very**

nation from whom he had stolen a colony, he was killed. His four years' rule must in the main be called creditable, and was especially acceptable to the Indians, the importance of whose good will he clearly saw.

In his place came Lord Lovelace, a favorite of the English court, who soon incurred the dislike of the people. Ten towns sent in a petition against unjust taxation, only to have their paper burned by the common hangman and to be told by their governor that "the people should have liberty for no thought but how to pay their taxes." Still the colony was not entirely mismanaged. The Hollanders were encouraged to mingle with the English and to adopt the customs of their rulers. The Indians were kept on friendly terms and their lands fairly bought.

But in the decade following the surrender of Stuyvesant the colony did not prosper. The trade with England did not equal the interrupted traffic with Holland ; wars in Europe prevented immigration and interfered with commerce. A letter to the Duke described Long Island as "very poor and inconsiderable, and besides the city of New York," said the writer, "there are but two Dutch towns of any importance, Esopus and Albany." New York city contained less than four hundred houses ; though it appears as a sign of progress that a line of post messengers was at this time established between that city and Boston, along paths marked by blazed trees.

New York again a Dutch Colony.—The Dutch Republic was now at war with England. Holland had already by treaty given up her claims to New York in return for Dutch Guiana (ge-ä´-na), and other territory much more profitable in those days than New Netherland had been. A large Dutch fleet coasting off Chesapeake bay in the summer of 1673 captured a vessel carrying some passengers from New York to Virginia. From these the Dutch learned of the dilapidated condition of Fort James, that the fort had but about thirty cannon and a garrison of seventy-five men, and that Governor Lovelace was visiting his neighbors at New Haven.

The fleet of twenty-three ships with sixteen hundred men aboard anchored off Sandy Hook and was joyfully visited by some of the Dutch citizens of New York. In a few days the ships passed through the Narrows and approached the city. Captain Manning, who had been, under Nichols, the first English commander at Albany, was now in the absence of Governor Lovelace in charge of New York city. He called upon the citizens for help; but many of them were now as anxious to go back to Dutch authority as they had been to leave it nine years before. They spiked all the cannon within their reach and gathered militia to help the invaders.

Manning demanded of Cornelis Evertsen, the admiral in command of the fleet, "Why do you disturb his majesty's subjects in this place?" and received in reply, "The place is our own and our own we will have." Manning asked for a day to think about it; he was given half an hour. When the sands of Evertsen's hour glass showed the half-hour, the Dutch gave the fort a broadside, killed some of the garrison and in return received some damage from the guns of the fort. Meanwhile some of the ships moving above the city landed six hundred men at the foot of the modern Wall street. This number was swelled to a thousand by eager citizens, and with Anthony Colve at their head they began their march down Broadway. The gutters of the street would soon have run with the blood of citizens capturing their own city had not Captain Colve met a messenger from Manning with an offer of surrender. After nine years of English rule, New York, taken fairly in time of war, was again in Dutch possession.

The Last of Dutch Rule.—The other settlements surrendered at once, and New Jersey readily came back under the sway of the troops at New York city, or rather at New Orange, as the place was re-named. The victorious admiral put the province under

military law and appointed the rough and pompous Captain Colve
as governor.   He was planning a government for the colony when
he received important orders from Holland.   That nation had, six
months after the capture of New York, made a treaty of peace with
England.   In this treaty each country agreed to deliver to the other
all territory captured during the war.   So when Colve had cared
for the colony for fifteen months, he quietly gave it up on the arrival
of the English officers sent to receive it.

The Reason for the Dutch surrendering a colony unfairly taken
away and honestly regained, does not plainly appear ; either they
had so promised before aware of the complete conquest of Admiral
Evertsen, or they feared that they could not hold the territory against
the encroachments of the neighboring English, or, as is most probable, they did not know the full value of a colony which had
already cost them more than it had returned.   At least, true it is
that England thus secured an uninterrupted coast line from Maine
to Georgia and made a United States possible.   "Our country obtained geographical unity."

Administration of Andros.—In November, 1674, New York

finally passed from the hands
of the Dutch to remain for one
hundred years an English province.   The Duke of York
tightened his grasp on the
colony; to cover all doubt he
secured a new grant from the
king ; he gave again New Jersey to Carteret and sent to New
York as governor, Major Edmund Andros, who, he doubt-
ed not, would be thoroughly
alive to his master's interests.

For ten years Major Andros

GOVERNOR ANDROS.

was busy with the affairs of the colony ; now he was penetrating into the far west of the unsettled Mohawk valley, viewing the fertile flats and making friends of the Indians ; now he was sending to Martha's Vineyard to assert the claims of the Duke. He assumed that New Jersey was still under his control, and went so far as to arrest Governor Carteret. He renewed the old contest with Connecticut, landed in force at Saybrook and demanded the surrender of the fort. Being refused he read the grant of the Duke and his own commission ; and when these selections did not soften the hearts of the Connecticut Puritans, Andros sailed sadly home.

VIEW OF THE WATER GATE (Wall Street) in Andros' Administration.

Condition of the Colony.—In 1678, Governor Andros while visiting England left on record an account of his colony. New York since Stuyvesant's surrender had doubled its eight thousand inhabitants; about three thousand of these were in New York city. This place was built up at the expense of the rest of the province by the bolting act, which for many years gave the city the sole right of bolting and exporting flour from the colony.

But its growth was slow compared with its progress in the nineteenth century ; at the close of the seventeenth century the northern limit of the city was a palisade wall, the present Wall street. Beyond this were a few houses here and there, a burying ground, and a few huge Dutch wind-mills; further on, farms, and then a rocky wilderness. A mile from the town, the law allowed wood to be cut; in the numerous ponds, fresh water fish could be taken; the hunting too was good, probably, for a visitor tells of treeing a bear in an orchard where Maiden Lane now is.

In the city itself, the fort was the first object that greeted the sight of the ships coming up the bay; within this was a church; and leading from it was a "Broad way." Within the corporation were numerous swamps, ponds and creeks, and there had been ill-smelling tanneries and slaughter houses, which were then ordered out of the city limits. North of the city, where the Tombs prison is now, was a lake known as the Fresh Water pond. Six public wells were dug in the middle of the streets, not so much for the bad-tasting water as for a protection against fire.

Long Island.—Two English visitors at this time tell how they were rowed across East river in the ferry boat; upon landing they went "up a hill, along open roads and woody places, and through a village called Breuckelen, (Brooklyn), which has a small ugly church in the middle of the road." They slept in the house of one Simon DeHart, a house still standing, and supped on oysters, veni-son, and wild turkey. They were surprised at the apples, peaches, grapes, and "great heaps of watermelons." All kind of fish abounded; oysters were plentiful; drift whales were frequently cast upon the beach of the island; while off the coast, whalers could cap-ture their huge game.

The Civilization.—In the eastern part of Long Island schools were well sustained; but elsewhere the children of the colonists were no better educated than under Dutch rule. Some of the peo-ple could afford to have private teachers; some sent their children to New England schools ; but the mass of the people were ignorant and superstitious. As a result many of the laws were barbarous ; stealing might be punished with death ; or the thief was branded with a T on the cheek ; stocks, pillories, placards and other means of exciting derision were common punishments. The Sunday laws were strict ; the Connecticut blue laws were scarcely more so. "No youths, maydes or other persons," said the law, " may meet together for sporte or play."

Trade and Money.—No pedlers were allowed to compete with the regular tradesmen of the place, except that Indians might bring in wood and long strips of bark for gutters or eaves-troughs. These neighboring Indians, in the great lack of servants, were often enslaved until a law of the colony forbade ; but the traffic in negroes thrived and the common price paid for a slave was one hundred and fifty dollars. Dollars and cents were of course not known ; and although large sums were reckoned in English pounds and shillings, yet Dutch guilders, Indian wampum and beaver skins were the common money in business. The bare necessities and a few comforts contented the people ; a little ready money went a long ways ; five thousand dollars was a fortune, while half that sum made a rich man.

The colony shipped from its ports, wheat, tar, lumber, tobacco and especially pelts and furs. On goods brought to the port of New York there was a duty of two per cent, if they came from England; while goods from other countries paid ten per cent. These rates were not so burdensome as were the taxes on property and produce ; which duties were established in the early days of English rule and still continued.

The Dongan Charter.—That these taxes and laws did not please the people their protests and petitions leave no doubt. Even Andros, ever a friend of arbitrary power, counseled the Duke to give the people a voice in the government. When William Penn added his advice, the proprietor yielded and promised an assembly. He did not trust this work to Andros, but giving him other duties, sent Thomas Dongan to be governor. Of Thomas Dongan it can be said, that he was the first governor of New York who had the

GOVERNOR DONGAN'S HOUSE.

breadth of brain and the trueness of heart which make a statesman. He first accorded to the common man of the colony his rights; ignoring petty quarrels at home and with neighboring colonies, he disclosed and combated the encroachments of the great enemy to English rule in New York and in America,—the French.

According to his instructions his first act was to call an assembly of seventeen from New York city, Long Island, Staten Island, Esopus, Albany, Rensselaerwick, Pemaquid, and Martha's Vineyard to act with the council of ten in forming a constitution. On the seventeenth of October, 1683, some seventy-five years after the discovery of New York, the representatives of the citizens adopted a charter for their own government. Other colonies had charters brought from England; this constitution was the product of

America. By its terms, "Supreme power shall forever be and reside in the governor, council and people met in general assembly." It secured the right to vote, trial by jury, taxation by the assembly, and complete religious freedom. By its order an assembly of twenty-one representatives was to meet once in three years; and in order to apportion the members the colony was divided into

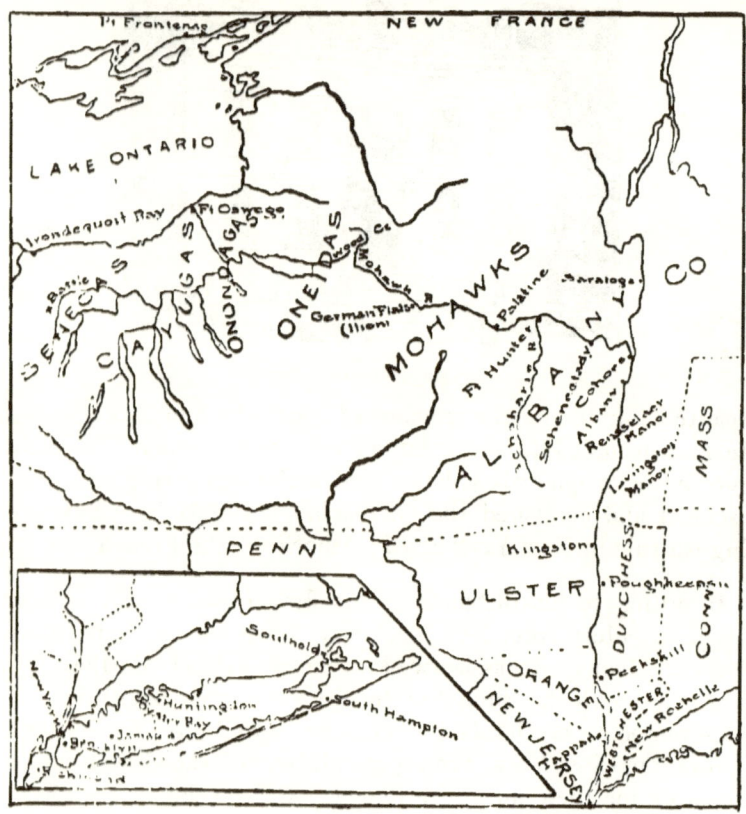

THE COLONY OF NEW YORK, SHOWING THE ORIGINAL TEN COUNTIES.

ten* counties : Suffolk, Queens, Kings, New York, Richmond and Westchester, which remain nearly as first constituted, and Orange, Ulster, Dutchess and Albany, which have since been divided.

The Charter Revoked.—Although this charter was ratified by the Duke, it was a matter of bargain ; for he stipulated that the assembly should in return vote heavy taxes. Soon he openly disregarded his pledge by levying taxes without the consent of the people. Two years after he agreed to the charter, by the death of his brother, Charles II., he became king with the title of James II. He then began to plot the complete subjection of all the American colonies to his will. He undertook to unite all the northern colonies except Pennsylvania under one governor. For this purpose he chose Edmund Andros and stationed him at Boston. Not finding Governor Dongan a fit tool he sent to New York one Nicholson, as lieutenant-governor under Andros.

Two Parties.—This quick destruction of their long sought liberty stirred up a rebellious feeling more fierce than the spirit which in earlier days prompted petitions and protests. But the people no longer were united in their action; they were slowly dividing into two parties. One class known as aristocrats or tories was made up of the soldiers and the many royal officers stationed in the colony ; to these were added many of the settlers, who grown rich were aping the customs and ideas of the aristocratic party of England. Against the combination of tories, governor and king, the party of the people, the democratic party, waged a long and determined contest. Bitterness was added to the struggle at this time by religious troubles. James II. was a catholic ; and he had ordered Governor Dongan to introduce that religion as the established form. But Dongan, himself a catholic, would do nothing

* There were twelve counties in the colony as then claimed. Duke's county included Martha's Vineyard and Nantucket; Cornwall county was Pemaquid, the land between the Kennebec and Penobscot rivers, granted the Duke with New York.

that was intolerant or illiberal. Still the protestants of the colony were too ready to imagine "Popish plots," some of them having suffered many things for the sake of their religion in the old countries.

The English Revolution of 1688.—While the colonists were thus stirred up about matters of religion and politics, they were more excited by the news that the English people after enduring for three years the reign of James II., had welcomed to their shores William of Orange, stadtholder of Holland, with his army, and had forced James to flee into France. This was the Revolution of 1688, a revolution without a battle, a victory of parliament over king ; for from this time parliament was supreme and the power of the king decreased.

The people of New York heard of the crowning of William with joy, the more because he was a protestant and a Dutchman. When they learned that the citizens of Massachusetts had put the unpopular Andros in prison they were undecided whether or not to obey Nicholson, he being the officer of the deposed monarch. All things were unsettled and the weak-willed Nicholson was not the man for the time. Such a man, however was found.

Jacob Leisler.—There lived in the colony a certain man, a native of Germany, a zealot in religion, of little learning. rich, brave, and an intense lover of liberty. His name was Jacob Leisler. To him, being a captain of colonial troops, came the dissatisfied band of militia which then happened to be on duty. They persuaded him to lead them in an effort to take the fort from the control of Nicholson. When Nicholson proved himself too weak to force an issue and sailed for England, Leisler entered the stronghold and took upon himself the duties of governor.

He was the first man who came from the people to rule the people. Rebel, fanatic and usurper he may have been ; patriot, hero

and martyr, he surely was. The council refused to act with him
and withdrew to Albany, where they resisted the force under Leisler's son-in-law Milborne, until forced by fear of the invasion of the
French from Canada, to admit the troops of the usurper.

Administration of Leisler.—The head of the colony styled
himself lieutenant-governor and was earnest and active in carrying
out the perplexing duties of the position. He sent an army against
the French who were invading the Mohawk valley and had burned
Schenectady ; he joined with the men of New England in an expedition by sea to Canada ; he improved the fort at New York,
planting about it a battery of six guns, which marks the place and
gives the name to the modern park, the Battery ; he sent evidence
of his faithfulness to King William and of his readiness to give up
the colony to the governor sent by his majesty. His mind saw
beyond the bounds of one colony and took in the needs of the
colonial brotherhood. He was the first man to propose a convention of the American provinces. But he was a century ahead of
the people.

Arrest of Leisler.—Meanwhile nearly two years of Leisler's
rule were past and the year 1691 came before Sloughter, the governor appointed by the new king arrived in New York. It happened that Captain Richard Ingoldsby, in charge of Sloughter's
troops, reached New York long before his commander. Ingoldsby
demanded the fort and was refused on the ground that he had no
authority to govern the colony. Leisler resisted a siege and
defended his post even to the shedding of blood ; but at the same
time he declared himself ready to give up his position when Sloughter should appear and present his credentials. And so he did. But
no sooner was Sloughter in office than the enemies of Leisler caused
his arrest, and in their bitter hatred secured a sentence of death.
When they seemed likely to be baffled by Sloughter's dislike to sign

the death warrant, they called to their murderous design the ready help of liquor, plied the governor with wine at a party, and from the drunken man obtained his signature.

Two days later, on a Saturday morning of May, 1691, as most accounts say, Sloughter lay in a drunken slumber. Without the rain fell and through its beating, Leisler and Milborne were led to the gallows. About them the people crowded ready to rush forward at their death and seize some memento. To the sheriff asking "if he were ready to die," Leisler answered "Yes." As the handkerchief was put about his face, he said, "I hope these eyes shall see our Lord Jesus Christ in Heaven. I am ready." Thus died the champion of a cause, which by his death was aroused to victory. With Bacon of Virginia, he was in spirit the ancestor of the Revolutionary heroes. Before the waning century was gone, his body was raised to lie in state, a royal governor did honor to his memory, and the parliament of England relieved his family and exonerated his administration.

AUTOGRAPH OF LEISLER.

CHAPTER V.

New York and New France.—For seventy years New York stood in the front rank of the English colonies struggling with the French for the possession of North America. New France, a name given to Nova Scotia, New Foundland, Canada and the valley of the Mississippi, embraced also, as the French would have it, that part of the present State of New York, from which the water flows into the Great Lakes and the St. Lawrence.

On the other hand the New York colonists claimed that these lakes and the river themselves were their northern boundaries, using the poor argument that Charles II. had thus specified in his grant. and giving as a much better reason that the land in dispute was occupied by their allies, the Iroquois.

French Missionaries among the Iroquois.—In 1642, some twenty-five years after Champlain failed to establish the arms of France in New York, Isaac Jogues, (zhōg), a Jesuit priest, scholar and traveller, was dragged from his canoe on the St. Lawrence by a band of Iroquois and carried to their towns on the Mohawk. He ran the gauntlet and suffered the keenest tortures; he finally reached New Amsterdam, went back to Canada and returned as a missionary to the Indians. With woods for a chapel and a cross cut in the bark of a tree he was the first preacher of Christ's gospel among the red men of New York.

Condition of the Iroquois.—The tribe among whom Jogues preached and soon suffered death was the Mohawk. These were the fiercest of the Iroquois and the tribe most friendly to the Dutch

(49)

and English. They lived nearest the whites, westward from Albany, along the river named from them. The Iroquois, however, had no fixed location, changing their villages as the soil was impoverished. A general idea of the situation of the Five Nations may be had from the five bodies of water and the four counties named from the tribes. The Mohawks long dwelt on the land of Montgomery county. At the extreme west of the " Long House," as the Iroquois termed their territory, were the Senecas, by far the most numerous of the tribes.

The total number of the Iroquois at that time could not have been much over ten thousand.* Of these, about two thousand were warriors, who might be found now on the banks of the St. Lawrence, and now sailing in birch bark canoes to the mouth of the Ohio. The old men, the women and the children remained in villages called castles ; these were composed of long, bark or framed houses, each holding many families and all surrounded with a palisade.

Progress of the Jesuits.—These towns soon after the death of Jogues were visited by many French Catholic priests, anxious to convert the savages, if might be, intent, at all events, on making the Iroquois friendly to Canada. One of the missionaries. Father Le Moyne (moïn) visited the Onondagas, there tasted a well which they said was infested with evil spirits and thus discovered the great salt springs of central New York. Le Moyne, at the deceitful invitation of the Indians, brought up the Oswego river a colony of fifty Frenchmen, who on the shore of Onondaga lake made the first French settlement in New York. This happened in the administration of Stuyvesant. But the adventurous band soon saw the murderous purpose of their pretending friends and fled. Yet

---

* There were in 1880, according to the census, about the same number of their descendants in various parts of the United States and Canada. The number, contrary to the general idea, is not decreasing.

on the whole the Jesuits made progress ; they met craftiness with
greater craftiness and gained converts while Dutch and English
preachers, who could not adapt themselves to the savage ways,
made little headway.

Invasion of New York.—The Jesuits were finally defeated in
their efforts to ally the Indians to the French by the fickle and
deceitful nature of the Indians and by the interference of the French
soldiers impatient of the slow progress of the priests. A foolhardy
company of daring men, in dead of winter of 1666 came up the
frozen Sorel and Lake Champlain ; but upon hearing that the
wide-awake English and not the slow-going Dutch then held the
fort at Albany, they quietly returned.

Still again in pleasanter weather of the same year thirteen hundred Canadians and Indians came over the same route and destroyed
the Mohawk towns. These were the first of the score of like expeditions, which made the name of the French a terror to the child
of New York, which undid the work of the priests, but which
extended little the borders of New France.

The French in Western New York.—After the expeditions
of 1666, there were twenty years of peace. Meanwhile the French
coveted New York ; and so much did the rulers of Canada value
the position of the English in the Hudson valley that they proposed
to their king to purchase the territory, "which," as they wrote,
"would render His Majesty master of all North America." Not
able to buy the Hudson valley the French governors determined
to try force once more upon the Five Nations. One governor on
pretense of making peace enticed to Fort Frontenac* (fron-te-nac),
a band of Iroquois and thereupon murdered some and sent others
to France as slaves Thus to break a truce was the blackest of
crimes to an Indian. and henceforth it was war to the knife.

---

* Fort Frontenac, the first building on Lake Ontario, had been put up by a governor of
that name to catch the trade of the western Indians. The city of Kingston now stands on
the spot.

Soon after, the Canadian governor landed at Irondequoit bay and defeated the Senecas in Ontario county, near the town of Victor; then sailing to the mouth of the Niagara river, he landed on the New York side, and built Fort Niagara. Thereupon Governor Dongan, unwilling to see the French hold this passage to the west, sent a protest, claiming the land to be "within my Master's territoryes without question." The Five Nations were more excited by the encroachment than Dongan, and without his aid they so harassed the little garrison that they were glad to escape from the new fort. The terrified fugitives did not stop at Fort Frontenac but blew up that stronghold and withdrew to the island of Montreal. Even here they were besieged by the Indians and all Canada shivered before the avenging fury of the Iroquois.

Frontenac.—At this critical period, Count Frontenac, once before governor of Canada and now an old man, returned to redeem the colony. Since Champlain, he was the most notable figure of New France. He could assume the paint and fury of a savage and yell with them in the war dance ; he could lead his troops through tangled woods, when from the weakness of years he must be carried in a chair. He now made peace with the Iroquois as best he could, and since war had broken out between England and France, known in the colonies as King William's war, he made ready to strike a blow upon the English.

Burning of Schenectady.—In the winter of 1690 he sent an army of two hundred, half of whom were Indians, over Lake Champlain. In the midst of a driving snow they came to the most westerly town of New York, Schenectady. It was eleven o'clock at night, and the Dutch inhabitants slept in the fifty or more houses huddled within palisades. The gates of the weak fortification were open, and no guards were there except sentinels of snow put up in play by the boys. The black forms moved silently until distributed through the place. Then there was a yell, the crashing of doors and horrid butchery. A few escaped in night clothes and froze

their feet in an attempt to reach Albany; some were spared; some
were kept for torture; while sixty, among them twelve children,
were fortunate enough to meet a speedy death. By noon the city
of Van Curler was in ashes, and the victors were hurrying on snow
shoes to Montreal.

Raids of the French and English.—Three years later a like
expedition frightened even the people of New York city, but succeeded simply in burning a few Mohawk towns and then returned.
After another three years Frontenac changed his course, entered New
York by Lake Ontario and destroyed the castles of the Onondagas
and Oneidas. The Indians took to the woods at the invasion of the
immense force, and but one warrior, a man of eighty or more years,
was caught. Him the Indians with Frontenac tied to a tree and
tortured with knives. "You had better," said he, "let me die by
fire, that these French dogs may learn to die like men." This
Indian was the only one killed by an invasion designed to extermi-
nate the Iroquois.

The small armies sent by New York and by some of the near colonies to beat back the French and to enter Canada accomplished
little. They either found the difficulties of march too great, or
quarreled about their leaders and disbanded. The most notable
leader of New York forces at the time was the mayor of Albany,
Peter Schuyler. He penetrated to the banks opposite Montreal
and gave the French a long remembered whipping. These excur-
sions back and forth were stopped by the death of Frontenac and
by the treaty of Ryswick (riz'wik) between France and England.

Queen Anne's War.—The treaty fixed no boundaries between
the colonies, and as the mother countries were soon at war again, the
children in America were quick to take up the quarrel. This time
it was resolved to drive the French entirely from Canada. In
1709 and again two years later large parties well equipped gathered

at Albany to march into Canada and to meet another party sailing from Boston up the St. Lawrence. The expeditions by sea were disgraceful failures, and the armies from Albany did not reach the head of Lake Champlain ; the result was a burdensome debt upon the colony. As the other colonies were shielded by New York, they were asked to help pay the expenses of the war ; but with a few exceptions they neglected to send money or men.

New York's Weakness and Strength in War.—The separateness and mutual jealousies of the English colonies were a source of weakness. The French, less in number, won by unity and push. New York was furthermore at a disadvantage in the contest on account of the quarrels with the governors, into whose hands the assembly feared to put a strong force. The farmer colonists too were not easily aroused to war ; but in the long run they were more than a match for traders, hunters and professional soldiers. Their families and harvests gave a steady increase to New York ; while the Canadian colony, depending largely for recruits and for bread upon the slow-coming ships from France, grew little in population and was at times on the point of starvation.

New York, moreover, was strong in the help of the Iroquois ; in fact the English presumed too much on their red allies and often, after promising help and supplies, left the Indians to fight alone. How the struggle would end was not then decided, for the war, known as Queen Anne's war, was closed by the treaty of Utrecht (u-trek). By this treaty the French acknowledged that the Iroquois owned the land south of the St. Lawrence and of the Great Lakes. And with this comfort New York turned to arrange her neglected affairs at home.

CHAPTER VI.

A HALF CENTURY OF ENGLISH RULE.—1691-1744.

The Successors of Leisler.—Internal strife had been bitter during the early struggles with the French. The two parties which had grown up in the colony were known as the Leislerians and the anti-Leislerians; of these the Leislerians or democratic faction was the larger; while the aristocratic party had the active support of the government of the colony. The management of affairs was not long in Sloughter's hands, for his drunken habits brought his death within a few months after the hanging of Leisler. He was followed by Benjamin Fletcher, a man of little ability but of strong passions, a poor governor but a good soldier. He moved his troops so swiftly up the Hudson to oppose the French that the approving Indians named him " Ca-yen-gui-ra-go,"—"Great Swift Arrow." He placed the enemies of Leisler in office and made offensive efforts to establish the English church in the colony. It was through him that Trinity church was at this time (1696) established. He was intent too on introducing the English language more completely; for although it was now thirty years after the surrender of Stuyvesant, the Dutch were still in the majority and their speech was the language of business.

New York Surrounded with Dangers.—During the seven years following 1690, the colony had its hands full with the war with France and the management of the Five Nations. These affairs Governor Fletcher was wise enough to trust largely to the skilful management of Peter Schuyler. New York seemed beset with difficulties; for about this time bands of pirates became a terror along the American coast. They were so bold that they even entered the bay and in sight of New York city captured merchant vessels and made safely off.

Probably the pirates were in league with officers of the government, perhaps with the governor himself. Captain William Kidd, a well known shipmaster, was sent against them. He took his well equipped ship, ran up the black flag and became the prince of pirates. He was afterward hanged and his fabled treasures have been often dug for deep down in the soil of Long Island.

The First Democratic Governor.—It was to suppress these robber crafts that the English government recalled Fletcher and sent in his place an Irish gentleman, the Earl of Bellomont. This change was however more important to the colony because Bellomont as a member of parliament had defended the deeds and character of Leisler ; so that upon coming to the colony he joined himself to the Leislerian party.

During his administration, which occupied the very last years of the seventeenth century, the assembly was dismissed and a new one called ; for the act creating an assembly first granted and then recalled by James II. was restored under King William. The members, then nineteen in number, were elected by the people for no definite time but held office at the will of the governor. The assembly might remain for years ; it might any day be dissolved. Over its acts the governor had an absolute veto. There was also a council of seven to twelve men, appointed by the king or governor, who had something of the power of a modern State senate, or as Governor Fletcher said, "they are in the nature of the House of Lords." The new assembly, elected in Bellomont's administration, was largely democratic showing that the sentiment of the colony favored the friends of Leisler. All things seemed favorable to the security of the common citizen of New York, when Bellomont died.

Cornbury.—After an interval in which the senior member of the council as lieutenant-governor had charge of the colony, Lord Cornbury, in the second year of the eighteenth century arrived at New York as governor; soon after, he became governor also of New Jersey.* Tyrannical in his rule, loose in morals, dishonest in business, he was the first of the grasping, insolent governors of New York who drove the peace-loving people to join in a war against the government of England.

The Assembly versus the Governor.—All the disputes between the people of the colony, represented by the assembly, and the government of England, represented by the governor, centered in the question of taxation. As the Revolution of 1688 in England had established the principle that the people can be taxed by their

NEW YORK CITY IN 1704.

*The proprietors of New Jersey at this time surrendered their claims to the crown, and for thirty-six years that province, although keeping its own assembly, was under the governor of New York.

representatives only, so the assembly of New York, chosen by the citizens, assumed and maintained that they alone could tax the people of New York. They submitted to the Navigation Laws which exacted revenue from the ocean trade, but they themselves imposed all internal taxes. Here lay the advantage of the colony in the struggle against the despotic power of the rulers. No fixed amount was paid the governor but bountiful sums were voted for a year or for a term of years for his support. As Cornbury, like many other governors, took the place for the money in it, if the assembly wished his signature to a bill or his order to carry out any project, they withheld the revenue until he came to terms. "We must surrender once a year," said a disgusted governor of New York.

The Assembly Takes Control of the Revenue.—Then the people took another step toward freedom. They had at first given money to the governor to lay out as he thought best; later they named the items and the amounts to be applied to each object. At one time the assembly voted seven thousand dollars* to erect forts at the Narrows, where Forts Hamilton and LaFayette now stand. The money disappeared in Cornbury's pocket. Then the assembly appointed a treasurer; and thenceforth the governor could get but the sums voted him. These amounts were not small; the salary of a governor was generally from five thousand to ten thousand dollars. This was a small part however of his revenue; since appropriations for various items were lavishly given, Cornbury receiving nine thousand dollars for his expenses in crossing the ocean. During this man's administration the people advanced more rapidly toward freedom than under the favorable rule of Bellomont. The two warring political factions united in one party of opposition to the governor.

---

* Money was raised largely by poll tax; this tax was not equal for every man, but about as follows, changing English money to a similar amount in United States currency: Every freeman between sixteen and sixty, 18 cents; bachelors over twenty-five years of age 55 cents; a man wearing a wig $1 10; a lawyer, $5; a member of assembly $10.

The leading men of the colony at this time were Peter Schuyler*, William Smith, Lewis Morris and Robert Livingston.   Three of these men, Schuyler, Morris and Livingston, were of families renowned in American history; two, Morris and Livingston, were the grandfathers of signers of the Declaration of Independence.

PETER SCHUYLER.

* Peter Schuyler, a Dutchman, was the great man of early English rule.   He was made mayor of Albany by Dongan, and for a long time was in charge of the Indian affairs of the colony.   Like Van Curler he had unbounded influence over the Iroquois by whom he was greatly admired.   He was known among them as Brother " Quidder," that being as nearly as they could pronounce Peter.   He married in the Van Rensselaer family, took a prominent part in colonial politics and for a time was acting governor.   His family was to gain greater renown during the Revolution from his nephew, General Philip Schuyler.

William Smith, an English immigrant, was long a leader of the party of the people.   His

The Last of Cornbury's Rule.—The administration of Cornbury is a chapter of unjust deeds. At one time the small pox and yellow fever raged in the city and drove him and his officers to Jamaica, Long Island. The Presbyterian minister of the place offered him his house. The governor managed to turn the parsonage over to the church of England together with the only meeting house of the village, one built by the Presbyterians. For such acts he was heartily detested by the people. He was in debt to many of the store-keepers of New York city, and when removed from office by his cousin Queen Anne he was thrown into prison until released by a timely legacy.

Governor Hunter.—This was about the beginning of Queen Anne's war and after one or two others had for a short time tried their hands at the helm, Robert Hunter came to govern the colony. In learning and in polished manners he was the ablest of the English governors; but he was unfit for the unpleasant tasks before him. The failure of the expeditions of 1709 and the following years angered the Iroquois and threw the colony into debt. To meet the obligations paper money was for the first time issued, and this soon became worth but a third of its face value. The assembly refused to grant revenue but for a single year, and withal Governor Hunter had little heart for a contest with that obstinate body. He took in the situation at once and wrote home,—"The colonies are infants at their mother's breasts, but such as will wean themselves when they become of age."

---

sou wrote the first history of New York, but deserted the cause of the people during the Revolution.

Lewis Morris, of Welsh parentage, was a native of New York. His father, a soldier in Cromwell's army, bought a tract of land near Harlem, calling it Morrisania, (sâ), now a part of New York city. Lewis Morris befriended New Jersey and was in 1738 the first separate royal governor of that colony.

Robert Livingston was a Scotchman who bought a tract of land south of the estate of the Van Rensselaers on the east bank of the Hudson and became one of the rich patroons or lords of the manor. He was appointed by Governor Andros secretary of the first board of commissioners of Indian affairs. He led the opposition to Leisler but later joined the cause of the people against the corrupt and knavish Cornbury.

The Population: Number.—A sturdy infant the colony was already. The opening of the new century found 20,000 inhabitants. At the quarter, (1725), the number was twice as many,—40,000 ; at the half century the number was again doubled, and when another twenty-five years brought 1775 and the close of English rule, the population, doubled again, was 160,000.*

Distribution.—The people were filling the Hudson valley, spreading over Orange and Ulster counties and further north they were looking longingly to the land where the Mohawk would easily carry them. In this valley Schenectady was long the last town ; the land beyond, which remained unsettled from fear of the French and their Indian allies, was known as the Indian country. But nothing could long keep the settlers from tilling this rich low-lying land. They planned to possess the hunting grounds of the Iroquois, they cheated and maddened the savages at times, but they got the land.

A fort was built at the mouth of Schoharie creek and named from Governor Hunter. This officer with a visionary and costly scheme of colonization brought to America three thousand Germans from the persecuted district of the Palatinate (pa-lat′-i-nate). Some of these people, disappointed in the places provided for them along the Hudson, pushed westward from Schenectady and marked their settlements with the names Palatine Bridge and German Flats.

Occupation ; the Indian Trade.—The colonists were in these times largely farmers ; still sailors and fishermen were a considerable part of the people of New York city and of Long Island; while many trappers and traders made Albany their headquarters and carried their dangerous business as far as Lake Superior. In this Indian trade the French had the advantage of position ; but the English at Albany could afford to give the Indians nearly twice as

* The exact figures are, in 1703, 20,665; 1723, 40,564; 1749, 73,318; 1771, 163,337.—*American Cyclopædia.*

much powder, rum and woolen cloth for a beaver skin as they could get at Montreal or Fort Frontenac. The colony of New York planned to fortify a position on Lake Ontario in order to compete with Fort Frontenac for the trade with the western Indians; and after a long delay, in 1722, at the mouth of the Oswego river, a storehouse and later a fort were built where now is a populous city.

Governor Burnet and the French.—This important step was

taken by Governor William Burnet, who two years before received the place of the gifted but discontented Hunter. The name of Burnet may be added to the short list of liberal-minded and public-spirited foreign governors of New York. He perceived that the design of the French was to secure North America; he attempted to unite king and colonists in preoccupying the banks of the Ohio and Mississippi with a line of English forts. But the king, three thousand miles away, did not realize the situation; while the colonists, intent on scraping and hoarding, were so fearful of taxation that they would not permit a saving outlay of colonial money.

GOV. BURNET.

Burnet, himself, as French writers confess, left no stone unturned to defeat the projects of France. He called a council of colonial governors at Albany, the first of the many conferences held at that place with the Six Nations.* He attempted to pass beyond Oswego

---

* The Iroquois a short time since had received the Tuscaroras, the tribe of Powhatan and Pocahontas, from Virginia, and had given them land on the south east end of Oneida lake. The confederation was henceforth known as the Six Nations.

and fortify the deserted French position at Niagara ; but he was disappointed and was compelled to see the French a third time, in
1726, build Fort Niagara.

The French Trade.—Still nothing more than sharp letters
between the governors disturbed the peace of New York and Canada. The traders of Montreal had found that they could buy
at Albany cheaper than they could import from France ; so a brisk
trade was going on between the two colonies by means of Indian
carriers over the Champlain route. It was profitable business for
the merchants of New York, but it promised evil to the colony ; for
in the path of the traders the French were creeping up the Sorel,
up Lake Champlain ; soon they would be on Lake George and a
step would take them to the upper Hudson valley.

Governor Burnet saw the danger and induced the assembly to
prohibit the trade. For this act he was disliked by the merchants
of New York and London who used all means to secure his removal.
He further lost popularity by continuing the court of chancery, a
court of supreme authority, instituted by Hunter, which encroached
upon the power of the assembly. The governor also unfortunately
incurred the displeasure of Peter Schuyler and of Stephen De
Lancey ;* and thus a combination of influences brought about the
removal of the efficient but indiscreet Burnet to Massachusetts ;
and following this the trade with Canada was soon renewed.

Cosby.—When the next governor died after a term of a few
months, Rip Van Dam, the oldest member of the council, took the
office of acting governor until the arrival of Colonel William Cosby,
in 1732, a year memorable for the birth of Washington. As Cornbury stands in contrast with Bellomont, so Cosby is odious in comparison with the high-minded Burnet. When allowed to have his
own way, Cosby exercised his tyranny with offensive overbearance ;

---

* Stephen DeLancey was the leading man among a company of French Huguenots, who
to escape persecution in France settled in New York city and at New Rochelle.

when thwarted by the assembly, he bowed servilely before them He at once sued the popular leader, Rip Van Dam, and tried to force him to give up half of the salary of the year when he acted as governor. He deposed Lewis Morris from the office of chief justice; he quarreled with William Smith, the principal lawyer of the colony. He had cunningly induced the assembly to vote taxes for five years and so placed himself partly beyond the reach of public displeasure, except as it might be talked in the tavern or published in the newspaper.

The First Printer.—The press was then a new force in securing the popular rights of New York. Forty years before and two years after the death of Leisler, Governor Fletcher, feeling the need of printed laws and other legal papers, persuaded one William Bradford, a printer of Philadelphia, to bring to New York his rude printing press. He took this first machine of its kind into the province and for fifty years did the public printing.* In 1725 he began the first newspaper, the New York Gazette, a weekly paper about the size of a sheet of foolscap.

Zenger; His Arrest.—Naturally the paper of the public printer supported the governor; and quite naturally too an opposition paper was started; it was conducted by Peter Zenger, a former workman of Bradford. His paper, the New York Weekly Journal, was filled with criticisms and jingling rhymes aimed at the hated governor. Cosby fumed at the hard hits given him and arrested Zenger for libel. The publisher then edited the paper in his cell and sent for William Smith and another lawyer to defend him. The governor thereupon caused these lawyers to be deprived of the rights of attorneys. Zenger's next move was to engage Andrew Hamilton, a lawyer of Philadelphia, one of the ablest advocates in

* One day a boy of seventeen, a runaway apprentice from Boston, came to his office. Bradford did not have work for another hand, and so directed the young man to his son, a printer in Philadelphia. By this chance, Pennsylvania and not New York became the home of the statesman and scientist, Benjamin Franklin.

America. The case rapidly became famous. In the city a society of men, among whom were William Smith, William Livingston and John Morrin Scott, was formed under the name of "Sons of Liberty;" and in other colonies the inhabitants were intently watching the result.

The Trial.—Hamilton in opening his client's case made it plainly the cause of the whole people, declaring to the jury that they were to decide the question of freedom of speech and of the press against the will of a dictator. The judge, the tool of Cosby, charged the jury to bring in a verdict of guilty. Their verdict was, —*not guilty*. Amid uncontrollable applause Hamilton was borne from the room, given a banquet and placed on the barge for Philadelphia with firing of cannon. It was a great victory for New York and her sister colonies. Thereby the press became free and continued to be a most important aid in securing the rights of Americans until men laid down the pen to put an end to the contest with the sword.

Change of Governor.—The trial of Zenger was in 1735; Cosby died the next year, after providing that Rip Van Dam should not act as governor during the usual interval preceding the appointment of a chief officer. By this arrangement, George Clarke, a favorite of the aristocracy, became acting governor, and, by representing to the powers across the ocean that the place was ill-paid and beset with troubles, he kept charge of the government for seven years.

A Declaration of Independence.—At the beginning of his administration the assembly met him with a firm front. When they received from him the customary address or message, they returned a reply as was usual. They used none of the fulsome praise often found in these response... put the case to Clarke in plain terms: "You are not to expect that we either will raise sums unfit to be raised, or put what we shall raise into the power of a governor to misapply." They determined that henceforth they would not raise a revenue " for any longer time than one year; nor do we think," said they, " it convenient to do that until such laws are passed as we conceive necessary." To these words the politic Clarke bowed, bargained to support certain measures of the assembly and secured an ample revenue.

Public Plunder.—The revenue seemed to be his main concern. He came from England to be secretary of the colony; he returned worth $500,000,—a fabulous sum in those days. Nor does it appear that some other governors were far behind him in getting rich. They took large fees for land grants and titles; they appropriated broad tracts of land and sold it or distributed it among favorites; they took pay from merchants and from other interested persons in return for favoring some regulation of trade. Many of these transactions, which to-day would be thought scandalous, were then looked upon as the rightful income of the governor's office. One great political job of that time was the bringing of five hundred highlanders from Scotland to people the land about Lake George as a protection against the French. The project failed; but the Scotch mingled with English, Dutch and Germans, making for New York a broad-minded population.

The Negro Plot.—During the administration of Clarke, the colony passed through affliction. The winter of 1741 was severely cold and was accompanied with suffering. The citizens of New York city expected each day to see a war ship of Spain, with which nation England was then at war. The city was now a place of ten thousand people,—a fifth of whom were negro slaves. As summer followed the cold winter, rumors of a slave riot filled the air. It was no new sensation; thirty years before, the negroes were charged with combining for the burning of the city, and on very poor evidence nineteen of them were hanged. Since then the people had lived in fear of a conspiracy of slaves, and according to law when they found three negroes together they might give them forty lashes on the bare back.

In the fateful year of 1741 a few small fires occurred about the same time, probably set for the sake of plunder ; and in this the fearful citizens saw a bold " negro plot " to burn the city and murder the white people. Rewards for information were freely offered ; and the Dutch taverns were filled with gossiping, tale-inventing men, who manufactured a childish fear and foolish hatred of the negro. The people were seized with a panic and many fled from the city as from a pestilence.

After much search for the guilty persons, an ignorant girl, Mary Burton, was arrested in a drunken den on the suspicion that she knew the secret of the plot. In her fright she invented wild stories which were eagerly believed. Others in turn acknowledged a plot, and soon this was found to be the easiest way of escape. Informers became plentiful ; sheriffs and hangmen were busy ; the people grew more frantic and less sensible ; but not one reasonable fact was found concerning the origin of the fires.

Finally the fury spent itself after nearly two hundred people, mostly negroes, had been put in prison. Of the black men many were hanged, more were transported to the West Indies, while fourteen suffered the barbarism of a death by burning. Four of the white prisoners were also hanged,—among them one John Ury, a Catholic priest, whose religion seemed to deny him the consideration of his fellow citizens. The disgusting negro panic of New York city is a parallel to the witchcraft delusion of Salem.

Admiral Clinton.—Soon after these events Lieutenant-Governor Clarke closed his seven years' administration and gave way to Cosby's successor, Admiral George Clinton. With him the assembly began the old fight ; they were told to place a revenue and the militia unconditionally in the hands of the governor, since war with France was threatening. They flatly refused. They further declared that an assembly should hold office for seven years at the most,—a term then and now the limit of the English parliament. But soon these quarrels were overshadowed by the strife with France. The time had come to decide whether the French or the English were to govern North America.

CHAPTER VII.

THE FINAL STRUGGLE WITH FRANCE.—1744-1760.

King George's War.—From the treaty of Utrecht to the year 1744, there were thirty years of nominal peace; then broke out the struggle known as King George's War. It was the same story: raids by the Canadians over the Champlain route, great expeditions planned and equipped by the English and never carried through. This time the French entered Massachusetts, came within forty miles of Albany, burned the northernmost settlement, Saratoga,* murdered many and carried terror to the entire frontier. That the advance posts in New York were ill protected was due to the jealous fears of the assembly, rather than to any inactivity of Governor Clinton. The suspicion that he would misuse their men and money was their only excuse for failing to ward death from the hardy settlers and for breaking faith with the Indian allies.

The French West of New York.—Peace came in 1748 when no peace was possible. The French read the treaty to suit themselves; they built a fort south-west of the site of Dunkirk on Lake Erie, they strengthened Fort Niagara, they fortified a post at Ogdensburg, they extended the long dreamed of line of works down the Ohio and the Mississippi ; soon they would creep over the Alleghanies and threaten the narrow coast strip of scattered English settlements. The time was critical for the exposed State of New York ; the Mohawk valley was not safe ; Albany was threatened ; the harbor of New York would be the first great prize.

---

*The settlement contained about thirty houses and was on the Hudson near the present Schuylerville. The Saratoga of this war and f the Revolution was about twelve miles east of Saratoga Springs.

The Albany Convention.—To consider these matters and to confer with the Iroquois a congress of the colonies was called by the English government to meet in Albany in 1754. Hither came representatives from the four New England colonies, from Pennsylvania, and from Maryland, to meet William Smith, Colonel Johnson and others from New York, together with Lieutenant-Governor DeLancey, who since the departure of Clinton was in charge of the colony. Here came the Iroquois to chide the colony for their neglect; and among them was their great chief Hendrick,* whose speech has come down to

WESTERN NEW YORK AND PENNSYLVANIA IN THE FRENCH AND INDIAN WAR.

us as a model of oratory. Here Benjamin Franklin proposed a plan for a union of the American colonies. The proposal did not please the king : it seemed at the time to awaken no response from the colonies.

The French and Indian War: First Year.—The next year, 1755, the war opened in earnest. Troops began to gather at Albany. At the opposite end of the State was Fort Niagara with its garrison of thirty disheartened Frenchmen. Against them Shirley, the royal governor of Massachusetts, led two thousand men to capture the fort and to join Braddock marching from Virginia. Shirley heard of Braddock's disastrous failure to take Fort DuQuesne (du kane), reached Oswego, built ships, waited for fair weather, and leaving re-enforcements at Oswego went disgracefully back to the Hudson.

* Soi-en-ga-rah-ta, or King Hendrick as he is known to history, held the sway of a monarch over the Iroquois. He was a Mohawk, and at this time an old man; in his earlier days he went to England with Peter Schuyler and was there received by Queen Anne as one of royal blood. He was killed the next year after his speech at Albany, in the battle near Lake George.

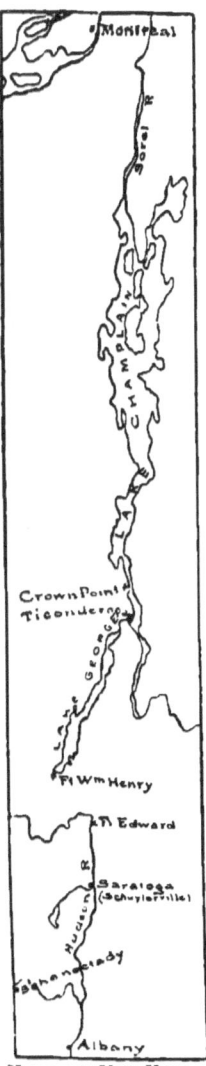

Here fifty miles above Albany, where the river turns westward to catch the torrents of the Adirondacks, Fort Edward was built as the advance guard of the English settlements. Thence it is but a short distance over a gentle rise to water flowing into the St. Lawrence. In the Champlain valley the advance post of the French had been for twenty years at Crown Point. With this point in view William Johnson, with over three thousand men, started north from Fort Edward, met the enemy at the head of the water, to which he gave the name of Lake George, and defeated them.* Without attempting to go further he loitered away the summer erecting Fort William Henry, the first building on Lake George. At the same time the French were pushing southward and building Fort Ticonderoga.

Second Year.—The much vaunted and only success of the first year was no real gain ; and the campaign during the next year was directed to keep what was already held. Oswego was threatened. A force to relieve the garrison was criminally delayed along the way by the commander, Webb, a royal officer. Meanwhile a new leader, Montcalm, had brought courage to the French. One day he reviewed his troops at Fort Frontenac, the same evening he landed before Oswego, and in ten days he had the forts, many vessels and rich stores. Then to show

* A skirmishing party under Colonel Williams of Massachusetts was defeated and King Hendrick and Colonel Williams were killed. The latter made a will at Albany leaving money to found a school. That school is Williams College, Massachusetts.

NORTHERN NEW YORK IN FRENCH AND INDIAN WAR

the Indians that the French did not wish their land, he utterly destroyed the well-placed fortifications.

A Time of Gloom.—It was a politic move ; the Iroquois were already looking with suspicion upon the English people who were fast occupying their land. The Mohawks, Oneidas, Onondagas and Cayugas had already been to Montreal to promise to be neutral. It was a time of gloom in the colony of New York. Three thousand English regulars were in the province, mostly at Albany and New York city. There at any moment a family might be compelled to feed and shelter English soldiers. The colonists knew that such acts were illegal ; but in their fear of the French they submitted. New York levied taxes, raised money and fitted out companies of militia capable of doing efficient service. But they were despised by the English, and their highest officers were made to obey the lowest officer of the regular army.

Third Year.—Johnson's fort on Lake George now became a death-trap. The garrison was surrounded by French and Indians under Montcalm. Forced to surrender, the men gave up their arms and were allowed to go to Fort Edward on parole. As the defenceless men started, they were attacked by the Indians, some were stripped of their clothes, some scalped, and those who escaped ran panting into Fort Edward. Here, resting contentedly, was the imbecile Webb with four thousand unused troops.

Fourth Year.—During the following winter the length of the Mohawk valley was open to the French and Indians. Palatine Village was burned, forty people were murdered and a hundred and fifty carried to a fearful captivity ; while the English officers enjoyed their snug winter quarters. During the summer, (1758), 17,000 men, more than half colonists, the largest body of men that had ever gathered in New York State, assembled at the site of the destroyed Fort William Henry, under the English general, Abercrombie. The army sailed gaily down the lake to the short, swift stream which carries the water to Lake Champlain. There, while Abercrombie skulked in a saw-mill, his misdirected men fell before the walls of Ticonderoga.

The Chain Broken.—Final defeat now seemed the fate of the colonies and their king. At that moment a captain of New England and a force all American got reluctant permission to do their best. They hastened up the Mohawk, down the Oswego, across Ontario and took Fort Frontenac without a blow. The chain of French forts was broken. The storehouse of the west was destroyed. There were already other signs of success. Pitt, the friend of America, had become prime minister of England ; he had sent out General Wolfe, who had captured Louisburg, the great naval fortress of the French. There were other successes outside of New York : soon after the fall of Fort Frontenac, Fort Du Quesne, in Pennsylvania, was abandoned by the French.

The Fifth Year.—The end was near. The French, few and starving, successful by unity and dash, suddenly collapsed. In 1759, Sir William Johnson captured Niagara and the way to the west was open. The French deserted Ticonderoga and Crown Point to concentrate about Quebec ; and when on the Plains of Abraham the brave Wolfe conquered the brave Montcalm, and both died, New York and her sister colonies had needed rest.

The Result.—There was no question now as to the northern boundary of New York. But the war which made the decision broke up many families and left the colony with a debt of one and a half million dollars. On the other hand the farmers of New York had found friends and brothers in other colonies : they learned the unbrotherly feeling of the English ; and in their marches they had viewed fertile fields in unknown regions of the State. The fear of the French and their savage allies could no longer keep them from **the lands** north and west of Albany. The very forts became centers around which future cities and villages were to gather. About Fort Schuyler Utica was to grow ; Fort Stanwix was the nucleus of Rome. Fort Presentation nourished the germs of Ogdensburg. The war with its terrors had yet many helpful lessons for the English colonies in America.

CHAPTER VIII.

CONDITION OF THE COLONY TOWARD THE CLOSE OF ENGLISH RULE.

The New York of 1760 and 1770 was no longer a collection of settlements; it was fast taking on the form of a State. The shape of its peopled territory was that of a letter Z; the Mohawk valley and Long Island are the upper and lower lines of the letter; the Hudson valley is the connecting bar.

The Island Counties.—Long Island was divided into counties as now, with Suffolk at the eastern end. The inhabitants here were largely from New England; they preserved their Puritan ideas and manners and much preferred to be a part of Connecticut.* Huntingdon, Brookhaven, Southampton and Southold were the principal towns.

Passing into Queens county the Dutch element became noticeable. Further on, Kings county also had its present limits, but its cities were hardly begun. Lower New York was not so crowded nor ferry passage so safe and rapid as to give an impetus to the growth of Brooklyn, so that it was still a village smaller than neighboring towns which are to-day enclosed within its spreading boundaries. The Dutch element prevailed in Kings county and grew rich in market gardening. Staten Island composed the Richmond county of those days also; but there were few settlers, except here and there a Dutch or French farmer and "one poor, mean village," Richmond.

* New England customs prevail on the east end of Long Island to-day; and indeed it would be more convenient for the people to sail up the Connecticut than up the Hudson to their capital city. Read, "A New England Colony in New York."—*Harper's Magazine*, Vol. 71,

New York County.—Turning northward, the island of Manhattan, with Bedloe's, Governor's, Blackwell's and other islands of the bay and East river comprised the city of New York. The city itself was then about a mile long and a half-mile wide; and its crooked streets extended to the present city hall. Beyond, the " Broadway " passed straggling houses and then stretched away as a country road among the farms which have since been given up to the great retail trade of the continent. The business centre of those days was Hanover Square : while the place for a fashionable residence was lower Broadway or Wall street.

" In the city," says McMaster, " scarce a street was paved, and these few were so illy done that Franklin observed that a New Yorker could be told by his walk as he shuffled over the smooth pavements of Philadelphia." The streets were crooked ; Pearl street had been extended along the line of the cow-path to the common pasture. Where City Hall park is, was a much larger common known as the " Fields," and further north, now without a trace, was a large fresh water pond, where the city fisherman often tried his luck.

Population and Importance.—The number of people then in the city was from twenty thousand to twenty-five thousand, being a seventh or an eighth of the population of the entire province: whereas in later years the population of the city has been to that of the State as one to four or five. Then, New York county had but half the number of people of Albany county and no more than Westchester county. Yet the city, compared with the rest of the State, was more important than now ; it was the capital during colonial times, the centre of all trade,—except the Indian traffic of Albany,—and it was the social metropolis. The brilliant events of society were not excelled by those of London, testifies a royal governor : while a local writer says that the people aped all the absurd customs of the English capital about the time they had died out in that city.   Dutch manners, however, largely prevailed and a knowledge of that language as well as of the English was necessary for doing business.

Religion.—The Dutch ministers still preached in their language

to diminishing congregations, who were beginning to prefer the English preachers. Yet the descendants of the old settlers clung to the mother tongue, and in one of the Dutch Reformed churches the services were in Dutch until the year 1803. This denomination, since English occupation, had given way to the Episcopalian as the favored church of the royal officers; and the Presbyterians had grown strong from New England recruits.

Durcn Church Built in 1693.

These denominations had two or three churches each.   The Baptists and Methodists, who had been worshiping in upper rooms in William street, built their first churches soon after the French war. A Quaker and a Lutheran meeting house and a Jew's synagogue went to make up the eighteen places of worship in the city which now contains nearly five hundred church buildings.

There was no Catholic church ; in fact at one time in English rule it was a crime of death for a Catholic priest to be found in the province. For a while Quakers and Jews were not allowed to vote; McKemie, a minister, was unsuccessfully prosecuted for using other services than those of the prayer-book. The early English governors had as a rule been more intolerant in religious matters than the Dutch rulers ; but the spirit of religious freedom was growing, and was soon to be fully recognized in the State constitution.

Public Buildings and Schools.—Beside the churches, New York had few public buildings. There was an alms-house, a city hall two stories high, an exchange, and a hospital, just begun and completed in time to be used as barracks for the English soldiers. These were the beginning of the vast array of public and charitable buildings which now abound in the great city. One other notable

KING'S COLLEGE.

building there was, however,—King's College, now Columbia College. This institution was organized in 1754, at which time there were said to be but about fifteen college graduates among the hundred thousand people of the province. Princeton and Yale on each side had long prompted the colony to found a school for higher education. As the complaint was made that the New York boys returning from Yale were filled with advanced notions on political subjects, the friends of the king took care that King's College should teach a sentiment of submission to England. So the college officers were from the aristocracy; but among their first pupils were such boys as Gouverneur Morris and Alexander Hamilton.

In educating the mass of the people the colony under English rule made no progress compared with its material growth. In 1702, the assembly awoke to the need of a grammar school and sent to England for a "native born English teacher, of good learning, pious life and conversation and good temper." But the governors gave the matter of education little thought. Another step was taken in 1732, when a free school was established in which Latin, Greek and mathematics were taught.

The Southern Hudson Counties.—Leaving New York by the Bowery Lane, or the Boston road, the traveler passed through the Dutch village of Harlem and then crossed the Spuyten Duyvil (spi't'n di'vil) creek to Morrisania, the manor of the Morris family, —since 1873 a part of New York city, but then in Westchester county. Westchester was widely settled in those days, mostly by the descendants of the advance guard of Connecticut Yankees.

Across the Hudson lay Orange county, then including Rockland and reaching back to the State line. Even in those days it was noted for producing "the best butter made in the colony." In the southern part of the county the Dutch abounded and Tappan was the principal village. In this vicinity there was great uncertainty where the New Jersey line would finally run.

The Middle Counties of the Hudson.—Northward Ulster county was an immense tract joining Albany county on the north and running back to the Delaware river and the Indian country.

Along the Hudson were typical New York settlements of Dutch, Irish, French, English and Scotch. The principal village was Kingston with its hundred and fifty stone houses. The county furnished the colony with flour, millstones and beer. On the other side of the Hudson, Dutchess county began at Westchester, included the present Putnam county and reached to the modern Columbia line, then the southern limit of the Livingston manor. Poughkeepsie and Fishkill* were its two villages, though they were said to "scarce deserve the name."

Albany County.—The rest of the State of New York, settled up to 1770, was known as Albany county. The city of Albany showed by the shape of the three hundred and fifty brick houses that the people clung tenaciously to the old Dutch customs. To the west, Schenectady was another thoroughly Dutch town, with a wonder in the shape of a town clock. The fertile land here on the river sold for two hundred dollars an acre, and without manure produced full crops of wheat and peas. Further west settlements continued to the centre of what is now Herkimer county. But the traders pressed on up the Mohawk, at the modern Rome carrying their goods over an easy portage to the lake and stream which conveyed their wares to Oswego ; for at this time there was no road connecting Schenectady with Port Oswego. Northward from Albany the withdrawal of the French was followed by another stream of settlers ; Hoosac, Schaghticoke (skat-i-kook), and Saratoga were the villages in 1760.

Distance and Traveling.—From this end to the other extreme of the colony was then as far, counting the time taken for a letter or a traveler, as it is now across the continent. If one did not care to trust the uncertain winds and unfavorable tides, he could count on getting from New York to Boston by land in a

---

* Kill means in the Dutch, channel or river ; hence Kill van Kull or the Kills between Staten Island and Bergen Neck ; also Schuylkill and Catskill.

week. Letters for a long time were carried no farther south than
Philadelphia ; but later the mail service was extended through
forest paths to Charleston. Then a weekly mail to Philadelphia
was started ; and finally a wonder appeared in the shape of a stage
running between the cities in two or three days, advertising itself
as a " flying machine." with all the comforts of a canvas cover but
with no suggestion of springs. In wet weather the cramped and
jolted passenger could find exercise by helping to lift the wheels
from the mud holes.

Customs and Dress.—More often the citizen of New York
traveled on horse back. On horse back he went to church, with
his wife perhaps riding behind him. In church they sat without
any heat in winter except that of a foot warmer. Indeed, what a
stove is, few in those days knew. Many other household articles
now found in the poorest home were then known only to the rich.
The workingman had no carpets, no pictures, no books and papers,
except the bible and an almanac, which in those days was sold and
not given away, and which might serve his children for a reading
book ; he had no glass or earthenware, simply pewter plates. He
received for a day's work less money than fifty cents now amounts to:
and if with these wages he could not pay for his coarse food and leath-
ern breeches, he stood in fear of being thrown into prison for debt.

  The clothes of the common people were largely homespun, cotton
cloth being an expensive luxury. The elaborate style of dress
shown by the portraits of the day was worn by the few rich. The
huge wigs hanging down upon the shoulders were worn by men
and sometimes even by boys ; but they went out of fashion about
the close of the French war. The men rivaled the women in bright
colors. The following description is given of a runaway slave.
dressed probably in the cast off clothes of his master :—" Wore a
light wig, a gray kersey jacket lined with blue, a light pair of
drugget breeches with glass buttons, black roll-up stockings.
square-toed shoes, a white vest with yellow buttons, and red linings."

The Great Families.—The many negro slaves and the lordly families who kept them made the social life of New York before the Revolution far different from that under the republic. The lords of the manors had vast tracts of land, which, like the Dutch patroons, they rented to their farmers and over which they had almost kingly power. Among them were the Livingstons with their 160,000 acres in the present Columbia county, the De Lanceys and the Morrises. In the winter the feudal lords betook themselves to New York city, where they mingled with the families of the rich merchants and of royal officers. New York city was "a nest of families;" many of their names, as Beekman, Van Cortlandt, and Lispenard, are given to streets of the city. They were all intermarried, but were not prevented thereby from having frequent family quarrels.

Such aristocratic families were found in no other American colony, except in Virginia ; and in Virginia the great planters were Englishmen, while the lords of New York were of various nations ; the Schuylers and Van Rensselaers were Dutch, the De Lanceys were French, the Livingstons were **Scotch**. As a result these families were often found siding with the people against the royal governors of England.

The Governors.—Toward the middle of the eighteenth century the feeling toward the governors became such that the people had no regard for one who tried to do as nearly right as he could. The position was little sought for ; the changes were frequent. " While Virginia had twenty governors in the century before the Revolution, Massachusetts twenty-one, and Pennsylvania twenty-five, the executive authority in New York underwent thirty-three changes." Many of these were lieutenant-governors. From the administration of Admiral Clinton to Tryon, the last English governor, the colony was most of the time in charge of Lieutenant-Governors James De Lancey and Cadwallader Colden. Eight governors died in office ; one, of a despondent mind, finding after a few days residence in the colony how the assembly would oppose him, hanged himself to his garden wall.

The Ruler of Interior New York.—While the governors were losing ground, there was in the Mohawk valley a feudal lord who was coming to be, in his influence over men, the most powerful man of New York. Sir William Johnson, who obtained fame and his title of Sir from his victories in the French and Indian war, came to New York when a young man, to look after his uncle's lands along the Mohawk. He gained the love of the Iroquois, learned their ways, was made a chief, bought their land by the square mile, built a stone house, called his settlement Johnstown and became the monarch of the Mohawk. In this favored valley the making of the Empire State went rapidly on. For it was the farmers of the State, the great middle class, who gave us the New York of to-day. It was indeed the very countrymen of this Mohawk valley, who in the critical moment of the Revolution turned back the tide of British invasion.

SANDY HOOK LIGHTHOUSE. (First built in 1763.)

CHAPTER IX.

THE BEGINNING OF A REVOLUTION.—1760–1775.

As the first century of English rule in New York drew to a close, the people were beginning to think of themselves as Americans. The English, too, began to treat the colony as part of one great province. Heretofore they had adopted but one important measure bearing upon all their American possessions,—that is the navigation laws. But these acts, which were intended to compel the colonists to bring and send all their goods in English ships, had long been a dead letter; at the end of the French war, however,

they were revived and enforced, greatly to the hurt of New York's growing commerce. England was determined to have a fixed revenue from the colonies, partly to pay the war debt, but especially in order to pay the salaries of the judges and the governors and thus render these officers independent of the assembly.

Stamps.

A Stamp Act.—Parliament, no longer under the influence of Pitt, went further: They decided to levy an internal tax upon the colonies and selected, as the easiest tax to collect, a stamp duty. Accordingly early in 1765, they passed an act requiring the colonies to buy stamps, varying in value from three cents to thirty dollars, and put them on newspapers, almanacs and pamphlets, on marriage licenses, mortgages and other legal papers.

(84)

The people of New York had already sent in their protest.
"The spirit of resistance," says Bancroft, "was nowhere so strong
as in New York." They declared upon the authority of the constitution that to vote away by taxation the property of one who has
no voice in the vote is to deny him the very right of property. Not
only did they assert that the tax was illegal, they declared that
they would not pay the duty. But the English had little doubt of
easily compelling payment; and in order to meet any possible resistance, they had left, on pretense of further trouble with France,
a standing army in the colonies with headquarters at New York
city. Moreover at the time of the passing of the stamp act, they
had enacted a quartering act requiring the colonies to furnish
the soldiers with quarters, candles, wood, soap and drink.

The News of the double insult came up New York bay with the
first days of summer. Men talked excitedly in streets and in public places; they gathered in secret societies and planned desperate deeds, they paraded the principal streets with a copy of the
stamp act fastened to a death's head with the words, "The Folly
of England and the Ruin of America." The press of the city,
free since the days of Zenger, had much to do in moulding sentiment. "From denying the right of parliament to tax the colonies," the papers fell to doubting "its legislative authority
altogether." The Constitutional Courant appeared with the
motto, "Join or Die." These watch-words were echoed from Massachusetts to Georgia.

Organization.—The Sons of Liberty, the leading patriotic society of New York, suggested committees of correspondence with
similar committees in other colonies. The separateness of the
thirteen colonies was the great hinderance to union. New York
city and Boston were then as far from each other as those cities
are now from San Francisco. The colonies at once fell in with this
idea of the Sons of Liberty and were soon united by a system of
correspondence.

One of the first results was the calling of a colonial congress to meet in New York city. The hated stamp act was to go into effect on the first of November; the congress met in October, and the representatives of New York and of eight other colonies adopted a firm declaration of rights, a candid statement to parliament of the situation, and a respectful petition to George III., the new king of England. The thirteen colonies were now of one mind.

November 1, 1765.—When the morning of the first of November came, the streets of New York city had the look of Sunday. Shops were shut; bells were tolling; flags were at half-mast; bills were posted, saying:

Pro Patria

The first Man that either distributes or makes use of Stampt Paper, let him take Care of his House, Person, & Effects.

Vox Populi;

We dare

People early came pouring in from the surrounding country; the increasing throng frightened the stamp distributor so that he hastily resigned; then the crowd gathering courage determined to seize the stamps. But here they were baffled; for acting Governor Colden* had landed the stamps under guns and put them in the fort.

CADWALLADER COLDEN.

As evening came on, a solid column of citizens marched quietly from the Fields down Broadway carrying effigies of Colden and of the devil, which they burned on the Bowling Green. Then they broke open the governor's stables, seized his carriage of state and burned that. Thereupon getting bolder, the people marched up before the loaded cannon of the fort and vainly demanded the stamps. At this a few violent ones who could not keep within bounds broke open and pillaged the house of a certain Major James, an English officer who had said that he would " cram the stamps down the throats of the people with the end of his sword."

Repeal of the Stamp Act.—When the next morning came, the governor thought it best to proclaim that he would not allow the stamps to be sold and then turned them over to the mayor of the city, a man in whom the people had confidence. By the time that a second stamp distributor had resigned in fear, and ten packages of the stamps had been found and burned, the excitement cooled

* During the frequent changes and absences of governors, Cadwallader Colden was five times called to take charge of the government. He was now over seventy years of age, a Scotchman, and had lived in the colony for over half a century. He is to be remembered as the most distinguished of the early writers of the colony, his principal work being a history of the Iroquois. In political matters he favored the aristocracy.

down into a quiet determination. If newspapers were to be sent out, a marriage to be performed, or a ship needed clearance papers, the citizens sometimes delayed proceedings for a while, but finally ignored the duty altogether. When parliament heard of these things and learned at the same time of similar events in twelve other colonies, they knew that the tax was a failure, and in the following March they repealed the famous act.

The Liberty Pole.—The news of the repeal, coming back by the slow five to ten weeks' voyages of those days, turned the people to the extreme of joy. On the king's birthday in June the men of the city gathered in the Fields, erected a liberty pole, and inscribed on it—

"The King, Pitt and Liberty."

To the king they were thoroughly loyal; Pitt as the eloquent opposer of the taxation of America by England was their idol; but liberty had as yet no suggestion of independence.

A reaction soon set in. While the stamp act had been indeed repealed, the right to tax the colonies had been expressly declared. The quartering act remained and was offensively suggested by insolent bands of soldiers strolling about the streets of the city. On an August morning early risers discovered that some of these troops had cut down the liberty pole in the Fields. Crowds soon gathered, and in a fight between some citizens and soldiers Isaac Sears was wounded. But the pole was put up, and when a few weeks later it was found again on the ground, it was promptly restored. Finally after one more successful raid by the soldiers the Sons of Liberty put up an iron-banded pole which stood for years as an expression of their sentiments.

Non-Importation.—While a pole or no pole was the question in the colony, parliament was preparing to place duties on the tea, glass, paper and paints brought to America. Thereupon non-importation societies were formed to discourage the use of all

imported articles. The idea originated in New York city, already
the chief commercial city of America, perhaps excepting Boston ;
and soon many letters were going from colony to colony securing
unity of action.

The colonists, especially the Dutch of New York, were noted tea
drinkers ; but they even denied themselves this seeming necessity.
The people encouraged the wearing of homespun ; they looked with
suspicion upon one dressed in fine clothing, but considered a man
in a seedy suit with much favor. By such means the importations
from England largely ceased, and the London merchants clamored
to parliament for help.

Suspension of the Assembly.—But parliament was growing
angry under the refusal of the New York assembly to provide supplies for the troops in the city. Finally the English law-makers
voted to suspend the power of the assembly to pass any law until it
voted a supply bill. But the assembly declared the action of parliament unconstitutional and went on with its business. Then it
was dissolved by the governor ; but a new assembly elected in 1768,
in which were George Clinton and Philip Schuyler, was no more
inclined to yield. It was about this time that the names whigs and
tories began to be used for the two parties in the colonies.

Indian Lands.—Meanwhile there were serious difficulties in the
interior. The Iroquois were restless at the sight of the long trains
of immigrants, who, no longer fearful of the French, were moving
rapidly up the Mohawk. The boundaries of the lands bought of
the Indians were vague ; the titles were generally obtained after
filling the owners with rum ; the settlers claimed much that the
Indians declared had never been purchased. The Iroquois were with
difficulty restrained by Sir William Johnson from joining in the
war with Pontiac, which wrought havoc in the colonies to the south
of New York ; but finally they were quieted with new and more
accurate surveys, and were paid for the contested land.

Boundary Disputes.—Not even at that time had the dividing lines between the colonies been fully determined. When Nichols agreed with Connecticut that the boundary should run twenty miles from the Hudson, by some Yankee trick, it is claimed, the line was run out to a point on the sound but ten miles from the river. The boundary, after a hundred years of contention, was put back to the twenty mile limit, except that the little strip, which to-day indents Westchester county along the sound, remained to Connecticut.

The Contest with New Hampshire.—Following the lead of Connecticut, Massachusetts claimed land west of the Connecticut river, and by virtue of actual settlement secured a boundary as far west as Connecticut's line. Then New Hampshire claimed territory as far west as Massachusetts held, and, about the time of the French war, settlers with grants from New Hampshire began to occupy land up to Lake Champlain. After a time families from the Hudson valley came into the present State of Vermont, armed with deeds from New York. Settler strove with settler, and the two governors sent vigorous protests back and forth ; until finally, coming to no terms, the two colonies sent the question across the ocean for settlement.

The English government was inclined to favor the claims of New York, perhaps because the grant to the Duke of York gave a clear title up to the Connecticut river, but more likely because the English preferred to see the disputed territory under the royal governor of New York rather than under the chartered privileges of New England. At any rate the king decided that the New Hampshire grants, now known as the State of Vermont, were the property of New York.

A Tory Assembly.—For a while after this favorable consideration of the colony of New York, the contest with England was less bitter. The assembly of 1768 was soon dissolved ; reaction set in,

and the next year, when a new assembly was chosen, the strife was
one mainly of families and religions.   The Livingstons and Presbyterians were arrayed against the De Lanceys and Episcopalians.
The latter party was successful and soon showed its sympathy
for England by voting supplies for the standing army.   This action
called a storm of indignation from the people and led to a mass
meeting in the Fields.   The citizens, presided over by John Lamb,
denounced the assembly for "betraying their country."

It was a new experience for the assembly to find themselves
opposing the will of the people, and they showed as little discretion
as governors and councils had in like situations.   They summoned
Lamb before them, but could make nothing of his bold avowal.
They then took satisfaction in putting Alexander McDougal in
prison for libel.   On his way to jail he said, " I rejoice that I am
the first to suffer for liberty since the commencement of our
glorious struggle."   But he suffered little ; he was daily visited by
crowds bringing flowers and presents, and soon was released.

Battle of Golden Hill.—Shortly after this, the soldiers added
their part to the ill-feeling by throwing down the iron-banded pole
of some three years' standing.   This time they sawed it up and piled
the lengths in front of Montague's tavern, a resort of the Sons of
Liberty.   The usual mass meetings followed ; knots of citizens and
bands of soldiers gathered in the streets, and knock-down fights
were common.   At last the tumult culminated on a January day
of 1770, on Golden Hill, now John street, where a body of soldiers
and another of citizens happened to meet.   A battle of fists, canes
and cart-stakes on one side, and of bayonets on the other ended in
no immediate deaths, but caused blood to flow freely.   This fight
did much to take away regard for the mother country ; it happened
two months before the Boston Massacre and has been called the
first bloodshed between American patriots and the British soldiery.

Importation Resumed.—These exciting events did not please the farmers and merchants, who thrived better in quiet times. To them it was good news that parliament had taken off all duties on imports to America, with the exception of tea. Accordingly the merchants of New York city met and agreed to renew the trade in all other goods. New York had proposed the non-importation agreement, and alone, says the historian of America, "had been true to its agreement." In so doing the colony had lost five-sixths of its trade, while the New England colonies and Pennsylvania had lost but a half of their traffic, and other colonies had even increased their importations. Still the people of these colonies were angry at the action of New York. "Send us your old liberty pole, as you can have no farther use for it," said the men of Philadelphia. The Sons of Liberty joined in the same strain ; but when men went around from house to house to take the vote of the citizens of New York city, they found that 1180 to 300 favored the action of the merchants.

Royal Governors.—This was in 1770. In that year Lord Dunmore, another of the oft-changing magistrates of the colony, arrived. His short administration is noticeable for the fact that, according to instruction, he would accept no salary from the province, but received his pay from the quit-rents and colonial duties which went into the English treasury. When William Tryon, destined to be the last English governor of New York, succeeded Dunmore, the following year, he too took no salary from the assembly. Still Tryon did not rule offensively but rather was successful in quietly carrying out the requirements of the despotic parliament.

The Tea Tax.—The quiet times which followed were interrupted in 1773 at the news that the tax on tea was reduced to six cents a pound. As tea could thus be bought cheaper in the colonies than in England, parliament thought that an ingenious plan had been found to induce the Americans to buy the tea and pay the tax.

But the colonists saw the trick. At New York city they organized a society of "Mohawks," to prevent the landing of the tea-ship then coming to that port ; and while a like party at Boston were throwing a ship-load into the harbor, the Mohawks of New York waited in vain for their storm-driven vessel. When the ship finally anchored in the bay, it was not allowed to land ; but another boat succeeded in getting eighteen chests to the dock, which were found and in broad day dumped into the harbor.

Thus in all the colonies the final attempt of England to enforce taxation failed ; then parliament, changing its tactics, determined to reduce one colony thoroughly by force, and afterward to proceed to the rest. Accordingly it singled out Massachusetts, and closed the port of Boston. The other colonies were awake in a minute. Again in New York city the Fields held another crowd of excited men led by Lamb, McDougal, and Sears. This was known as the "Great Meeting." One of the eloquent speakers was a slight, girlish-looking boy, seventeen years old, a student of King's college. The listeners said to one another, "Who is he ?" and the word was passed around, "ALEXANDER HAMILTON."

Parties in New York.—New York sent words of sympathy to Massachusetts, but was much divided about what to do. There were three parties in the province. First tories who wished fair terms with England, but were intent on obedience at any price ; such were Colden, the DeLanceys, many of the church of England and those holding office under the crown.

At the other extreme was the party headed by the Sons of Liberty ; such were Isaac Sears, Alexander McDougal, John Morrin Scott, the workingmen and not a few of the rich. These men were bound to resist to the last ; they even talked of independence ; they collected arms, drilled, and were to New York what the minute men were to Massachusetts.

Between these two factions was a third party, the leading men of whom were merchants, lawyers and farmers ; they were determined not to yield the main point, yet hoped and sought for reconciliation with England ; such were John Jay and the Livingstons. This party was the strongest, as was shown by the meetings held in 1774 to appoint delegates to the congress at Philadelphia.

Indecision.—When this congress, sometimes called the first Continental Congress, took a firm stand in opposition to England, the assembly, which had long misrepresented the people of New York, refused by a vote of eleven to twelve to endorse the proceedings at Philadelphia. To add to the uncertainty of the time, the Sons of Liberty, joined by Massachusetts, bitterly attacked the moderate party for lack of zeal. Thereupon the king, getting his ideas through the royal officers and hearing of the action of the assembly, came to expect that New York would be loyal during the coming struggle. He had forgotten the New York of the stamp act time. There were indeed many tories in the colony, since there were so many royal officers. But at the same time there were many Dutch, Irish and French, with no ties to bind them to England. The merchants, too, were thought more desirous of money getting than of risking their property in opposition to England. But while they hoped strongly for peace, they had an unshaken determination to maintain their rights to the last. Moreover, Sir William Johnson was relied upon to carry the interior for the king ; but he was hesitating, and while he hesitated, he died. Of the final action of the mass of the people there was no doubt ; occasion only was needed.

Decision.—The occasion came on one Sunday morning, the twenty-second of April, 1775. As the people were going to church, swift riders flew past with the news of the battles of Lexington and Concord, three days before. The tory assembly never dared to meet again. Governor Tryon remained with what little authority he could hold until October and then betook himself to the man-of-war Asia, which hovered about the bay. English rule in the city might for a time be restored ; in the new-born State of New York it was ended forever.

SUMMARY OF EVENTS,—PERIOD II.

1664.   Nichols the first English governor.
1673.   Surrender to the Dutch fleet.
         Colve military governor.
1674.   New York restored to the English by treaty.
         Andros governor.
1682.   Delaware purchased by William Penn.
1683.   Dongan governor.
         Assembly called ; a charter formed ; the colony divided into counties.
1685.   The Duke of York becomes James II.
1686.   New York and New England consolidated as one colony.
1688.   English revolution of 1688.
1689.   Union with New England dissolved.
         Leisler usurps control.
1690.   Burning of Schenectady.
1691.   Death of Leisler.
1693.   First printing press in the colony.
1698.   Bellomont governor.
1709-11. Failure of the expeditions against Montreal.
1720.   Burnet governor.
1722.   Settlement of Oswego.
1731.   The French build a fort at Crown Point.
1732.   Public Free School organized in New York city.
1735.   Trial of Zenger.
1737.   Revenue granted for one year only.
1741.   Negro panic.

1745.	Saratoga destroyed in King George's war.
1754.	The Albany congress.
1755.	Beginning of the French and Indian war; battle of Lake George.
1756.	Capture of Oswego by Montcalm.
1757.	Surrender of Fort William Henry to the French. Massacre at Palatine Village.
1758.	Defeat of regular and provincial troops at Ticonderoga. Capture of Fort Frontenac.
1759.	Capture of all French posts in New York.
1760.	Navigation laws revived and enforced.
1765.	Stamp Act, November 1 ; Congress at New York city.
1766.	Stamp Act repealed. The liberty pole.
1767.	Duties on imports. Vermont decided to be part of New York colony.
1770.	Battle of Golden Hill.
1771.	Tryon governor.
1774.	Arrival of the taxed tea. Great meeting in the Fields occasioned by the Boston Port Bill. First Continental Congress.
1775.	Tryon, the last English governor, leaves the colony.

PERIOD III.

CHAPTER X.

New York in the Revolution.—1775-1781.

The Revolutionary war was simply the last of a long series of contests for political freedom,—a series in which were the first petitions for a charter, the Leislerian uprising against the aristocracy, the contest for an honest use of the revenue, the Zenger trial, the defeat of the Stamp Act, the non-importation agreement.

The Green Mountain Boys.—The men who first gained a victory over English soldiers in New York were a band of despised outlaws. The present State of Vermont had been declared to be part of New York. The New York government, however, had unwisely attempted to exact from the settlers of the New Hampshire grants a second price for their improved farms. Sheriffs were sent to enforce the claims; these New York officers met armed resistance and in a skirmish at Westchester killed a man and wounded others. In defense the inhabitants raised a band of militia called the Green Mountain Boys. They were led by such men as Ethan Allen and Seth Warner, for whose capture as outlaws the assembly of New York offered a reward of two hundred and fifty dollars each.

Just as a war between colonies seemed probable, news of Lexington came; and brave bands organized to fight colonists turned against a common foe. On the night before the tenth of May, 1775, Ethan Allan took eighty-three men across Lake Champlain from the Vermont side, surprised the English garrison, took them

(97)

prisoners "In the name of the Great Jehovah and the Continental Congress," and thus easily possessed himself of great stores and of that fortress for which large armies had fought. The next day Crown Point surrendered to Seth Warner; and in a few days Lake Champlain was in the hands of the patriots.

Choosing Sides.—The entire State was active. On the day of Allen's victory, John Jay, Robert R. Livingston and George Clinton, of New York, were assembling with the delegates of other colonies in the second Continental Congress at Philadelphia; companies of volunteers were drilling; British troops were leaving New York city for Boston, the seat of action. Colonists could no longer remain neutral; citizens found papers thrust before them upon which to declare which side they chose. Then it was evident that a majority of the people of New York wished to resist illegal taxation. Western Long Island did for a time seem to be under the control of the tories; and in the valley of the Mohawk, John Johnson, son of Sir William Johnson, was collecting a company of royal militia. But even there the patriots outnumbered them, and at Schoharie put to flight a company of men wearing red cockades and in the affray killed an Indian. This was an unfortunate incident; for the Iroquois were already inclined to side with the English and in the end a part of the Oneidas only aided the patriots.

Military Events of 1775.—The patriots of New York were called upon by the Continental Congress to furnish for the war three thousand men. By that congress George Washington, of Virginia, had been chosen commander-in-chief of the forces to be raised, and on the twenty-fifth of June, eight days after the battle of Bunker Hill, he passed through the city of New York on his way to take command of the crowd of armed men hovering about Boston. Philip Schuyler and Richard Montgomery of New York were also appointed generals; Schuyler was put in command of the army of the north with orders to protect the Canadian frontier. Further on he was directed by congress, contrary to the advice of wise generals, to invade Canada. But Schuyler falling sick turned over the command to Montgomery, a brave young Irishman, who, after gaining renown in Europe, had married a daughter of Robert R. Livingston and adopted New York State as his home. Montgomery, leading his men over the oft tried Lake Champlain route, took Montreal, joined Benedict Arnold marching from Washington's camp at Cambridge, and on the last day of 1775, in the vain charge upon Quebec, fell mortally wounded.

New York the Centre of Action.—With the failure of the Canadian expedition the first year of the Revolution ended. As the next year opened Washington held the English tightly in Boston, and independence was boldly talked throughout the land. When in March Washington drove the English from Boston, he knew well that they would next attempt to land in the large harbor of New York. So hastening his troops he arrived in New York city in April and began to fortify the poorly defended island of Manhattan. The city became a camp ; powder and muskets were made ; the awkward farmers were drilled ; tories were ridden on rails ; families who were able to get away packed what they could carry and fled. Washington had little hope of keeping Howe's 25,000 veterans from New York city with his 17,000 raw militia, poorly clothed, fed and armed ; but he intended to make the capture as costly as possible.

The Beginnings of a State Government.—Although armies were gathering, the organization of a State government was not to be neglected. The first step was a mass meeting at which a committee of a hundred was appointed ; the committee called for a convention of the representatives of the people ; the convention ordered a more permanent assembly to be elected. The first business of the assembly was to appoint a committee of its members to draft a State constitution.

. L. of C.

On the ninth of July this assembly met at White Plains to consider the Declaration of Independence, which a few days before the Continental Congress had published to the world. The news of the declaration was welcomed with delight at New York city; and the statue of the king was melted into bullets. The new State of New York gave assent to the declaration and was the first thereafter to receive in its borders the hostile army of England.

The English occupy New York City.—Before July was gone,

Howe landed on Staten Island; thence he crossed to Long Island; late in the month of August he met and defeated the patriot army in the battle of Long Island and following them across the river, in September, took possession of the city of New York. Washington did not at once leave the island but successfully fortified himself on Harlem Heights and at Fort Washington. This fortress was between the present One Hundred and Eighty-first and One Hundred and Eighty-sixth streets, "the highest point on the island and completely commanding the navigation of the river."

Washington, however, finding that he was likely to be surrounded, left a garrison at the fort and retreated into Westchester county. Here he was

THE LOWER HUD- defeated in an attempt to make a stand at White
SON VALLEY IN THE
REVOLUTION.   Plains, but was more successful at North Castle.

When he learned, however, of the loss of Fort Washington and all Manhattan island, he determined to lead his army toward Philadelphia; so crossing the Hudson at King's Ferry, he turned south to begin the terrible retreat through New Jersey and closed the year with the brilliant capture of a thousand Hessians. Washington never again led the main army into New York State for battle. Yet he himself and his officers frequently returned to the Hudson to cross into New England.

The **Hudson River** never completely fell into the hands of the English ; and thus that valley was ever a connecting link between New England and the other States. Indeed this river was, as in the French and Indian war, the key to success. The failure of the English to connect Montreal and New York city left the thirteen States a geographical unit. The English entrenched themselves at New York city, not merely because they had been driven from Boston, but because this was a great strategic point, a first step in securing the Hudson valley and thus in cutting the colonies in two.

Burgoyne's Invasion.—In accordance with this plan General Burgoyne was sent from England to Canada, thence to march over the Champlain route to the Hudson ; a second force under St. Leger was ordered up the St. Lawrence, over Lake Ontario and through the Mohawk valley ; while the English general at New York city was to move up the Hudson and meet Burgoyne and St. Leger at Albany. In the early spring of the year Burgoyne's ten thousand regulars, Hessians, tories and Indians were sailing up Lake Champlain. They easily captured Fort Ticonderoga and drove General Schuyler with his little army of the north back to Fort Edward.

By this time St. Leger had made his way to Oswego and was ready to lay waste central New York. With him was John Johnson and his company of tories from Tryon and Schoharie counties ; and there too was Joseph Brant, chief of the Mohawks with his band of Iroquois. This army, about two thousand in all, was soon at Fort Stanwix (Rome) besieging the little garrison. It was time for the farmers of the Mohawk to awake.

Battle of Oriskany.—The owners of the farms in the path of the English were mainly Germans, descendants of the Palatinates. Their commander of militia was General Herkimer. He called for all men between the ages of sixteen and sixty, and taking eight hundred men, armed with muskets and rude spears, set forth to help his countrymen at Fort Stanwix. The band of farmers passed the site of Utica and within six miles of the fort, at Oriskany, fell into an ambush.

After the first murderous volley from the hidden guns, the patriots sprang behind trees or turning back to back loaded and fired; though outnumbered they had no thought of retreat. Men fought with knives hand to hand; tories and their patriot neighbors were in deadly combat. For five hours the slaughter continued. There was no battle array to give confidence to the men; no beating of drums or floating of banners infused the inspiration of war. At last the Indians having lost their bravest chiefs fled, and the English retreated to the camp about Fort Stanwix. The field was left to the men of New York to bury their two hundred dead; for a fourth of their number had fallen in this the bloodiest battle of the Revolution.* Herkimer himself was mortally wounded.

Soon after this battle a rumor that Arnold was coming with help from the Hudson terrified the shattered invading army, and starting back to Oswego, they fled so hastily as to leave their arms behind. Burgoyne's expedition was doomed; its fate was largely decided at Oriskany. This battle " of all the Revolution " brings glory to New

Burgoyne's Invasion. York State. Here her farmers stopped the tide of invasion; freed from fear on the west they turned eastward to defeat Burgoyne.

---

* The number killed at Oriskany compared with the number engaged was larger than in any other battle of the war.

Surrender of Burgoyne.—He had already blundered. From Ticonderoga choosing the route by Whitehall and Fort Ann rather than over Lake George, he spent a full month climbing over the trees which Schuyler had left in his path to the Hudson. By that time militia had gathered increasing the American army to ten thousand men.

At last on Bemis Heights the armies met and in the two battles, called the battles of Saratoga, the forces of Burgoyne were first checked and then crippled. The credit of these victories was not to go to Schuyler, for Congress in a fit of impatience had put in his place the inefficient Gates; he simply carried out the plans of Schuyler and closed in upon Burgoyne. The English general held out in hopes of help from General Clinton at New York. But Clinton contented himself with going up the Hudson as far as Kingston, and after wantonly burning that town sailed back to New York city. Burgoyne, at last, cut off from supplies on the north, disappointed in help from St. Leger and Clinton on the west and south, and beaten back at Bennington on the east, surrendered.

The crisis of the Revolution was passed ; the States were still a unit. France saw the evidence of a strong people and offered her aid. From this time success in war, if not certain, was yet probable. The joy which filled American hearts at the defeat of Burgoyne could not be dispelled, during these last days of 1777, by Washington's misfortune at the Brandywine and at Germantown, by the loss of Philadelphia, or by that winter's sufferings at Valley Forge.

A State Constitution.—The same year marks the beginning of an organized State government. During the two years following the fall of the colonial government in 1775, the provincial congress meeting at various places along the Hudson had conducted civil affairs. One stern duty of those days was the expulsion of citizens hostile to the cause of freedom. Nor is it to be supposed that the tories were few and scattering ; they were especially numerous in the south-eastern counties.   There were more tories in New York than in any other State.   Such persons, if they were not thought deserving of harsher treatment, were banished to the English lines about New York city or were sent for safe keeping to New England.

The temporary State congress early in 1777, having assembled at Kingston, adopted a constitution largely the work of John Jay. This constitution called for the election by the people of a governor and of a legislature of two branches ; and though it allowed human slavery and required the voter to be a property owner, it provided fully for the civil and religious liberty of the common citizens.   The people now proceeded to elect George Clinton to be the first governor of the State of New York.   Thus a territory governed for a hundred and fifty years by lawgivers from Amsterdam and London came under the control of rulers chosen by its own inhabitants.

1778.—In the following year the English changed their plan of war ; they withdrew from Philadelphia and on their retreat to New York city were attacked and defeated by Washington at Monmouth. This was the last general engagement at the north ; henceforth the English directed their activity toward the southern States ; and while their army there was overrunning Georgia and the Carolinas, the force at New York city was content to plunder the towns of the coast during the summer and to spend the winters with the tory inhabitants in feasting and gaming.   Washington with his little army on the heights of New Jersey kept the enemy close to their headquarters.

But the latter half of the war, in which many of the northern States were free from disturbance, brought to New York widespread loss of life and property.   The operations in the State during these four years were of two kinds :—the Indian warfare west of the Catskills and in the Mohawk valley, and the incursions of the regular English army about the lower waters of the Hudson.

Indian Warfare.—Early in the season of 1778 the Iroquois, eager to avenge their loss at Oriskany, burst upon the settlements. Joined with them were many New York tories who, expelled from their homes, hacked down their former neighbors with more than Indian brutality. The settlements about Otsego lake were destroyed, Cobleskill and German Flats (Ilion) were burned; the Schoharie valley was laid waste; at Cherry Valley death and destruction culminated. There a fort had been built and a company of troops stationed. The little town of three hundred inhabitants was the most important of the scattered settlements along the upper waters of the Susquehanna, settlements extending then to the present limits of Broome county. Up this river in late November, when further attacks were not feared, hastened a band of seven hundred Indians and tories fresh from the Wyoming massacre in Pennsylvania. Walter Butler, son of John Butler, the rich and cruel tory of the Mohawk who led the raid into the Wyoming valley, headed this band of butchers. They cut down nearly fifty persons, mostly women and children, outside the fortifications; and while they did not capture the fort, they destroyed the village and carried forty prisoners away.*

Sullivan's Expedition, 1779.—The next year the patriots made a united effort to punish the Iroquois. From Fort Stanwix a company marched westward to destroy the Onondaga towns. Another expedition under General Sullivan was sent by Washington himself up the Susquehanna. To join this force General James Clinton, a brother of Governor Clinton, set out from Albany with a company of militia. They marched from the Mohawk to Otsego lake, and, damming the outlet of this for a while, floated down on the flood

---

* Fate had a fitting end for Walter Butler. When fleeing from defeat at Johnstown he was pursued by an Oneida Indian who " with a rifle ball brought him to the ground." " Butler now piteously begged for mercy. The Oneida brandishing his tomahawk replied in broken English 'Sherry Valley, remember Sherry Valley!' and cleft his skull."

to Tioga * and there joined the main body under General Sullivan. Thence together they marched westward, met the enemy under Johnson, Brant and Butler, near the present site of Elmira, and easily defeated them. At this point they turned north between Seneca and Cayuga lakes, destroying the orchards, cornfields and villages of the half-civilized Indians; they crossed the Genesee river and returning laid bare the country far and wide. Their deeds were not above censure; the result of the expedition was to make still fiercer the hatred of the Indians.

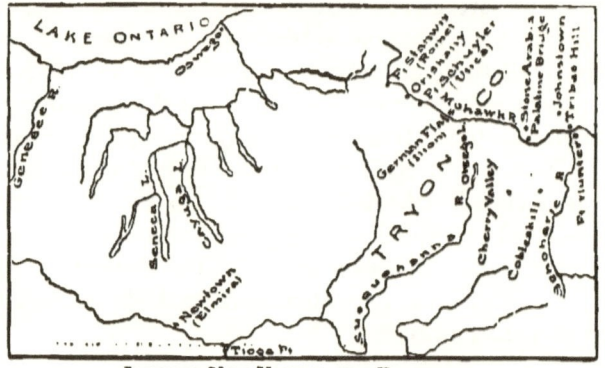

INTERIOR NEW YORK IN THE REVOLUTION.

During the last years of the war the Iroquois and tories terrorized the valley of the Mohawk to Fort Hunter and the Schoharie; they left their mark of bones and ashes at Johnstown, Tribes Hill and Stone Arabia; they even appeared among the settlers of Ulster and Orange counties. Before the slow-moving militia could reach them, they were gone.

Tryon county, which was then all of the State west of the north and south line of the Schoharie river, had at the beginning of this murderous warfare about ten thousand inhabitants. About a third of them, it is estimated, went over to the English; another third

* Now Athens. Pa., a few miles south of Waverly. N. Y.

were killed or disappeared.   When the awful deeds were over, three hundred widows and two thousand orphans were left to tell what the interior of New York did for American independence.

Operations along the Hudson.—The patriot citizens of Tryon county accomplished one great result in that they prevented the marauding bands of the enemy from passing the Catskills and falling upon the Hudson river towns.   That valley was the hope of America.   The lower counties overrun now by Americans and now by the English witnessed many stirring scenes such as are pictured by Fenimore Cooper, the novelist of New York, in " The Spy."

After the English General, Clinton, burned Kingston, during the Burgoyne campaign, and captured the forts further down the river, there was no operation of note until " Mad " Anthony Wayne appeared before the English fortifications at Stony Point.   Stony Point is a cape reaching out into the river below the highlands and commanding the stream.   Wayne in a brilliantly executed attack, planned by Washington, captured the fort and with a loss of fifteen killed, took five hundred prisoners, and destroyed the works.

A year later a sadder scene darkened this region.   A few miles above Stony Point, Washington had caused West Point to be fortified in order to hold the upper valley and to secure communications with New England.   Here he placed Benedict Arnold ; here the hero of Quebec and Bemis Heights became a traitor to his country ; here he wrote his letters to the English general at New York proposing to betray the works and the control of the Hudson ; here Andre met him to complete the plans.   It was at Tarrytown a few miles further south that three farmers, David Williams, John Paulding and Isaac Wart, captured Andre, the spy ; and across the river at Tappan he was hanged.

Andre's treatment was very different from that of Nathan Hale, who four years before, during the operations around New York city, was sent by Washington to gain information of the enemy.

Both men by the laws of war were justly executed. Hale was hanged the morning after his capture, was denied a minister or a bible or even the privilege of writing to his mother. Andre was given two weeks to prepare his defence, and was treated with every courtesy. The contrast between the two scenes did not serve to bring the Americans into a better feeling toward the English. If anything was needed to remove all further love for the mother country, it was the treatment received by the patriot prisoners in New York city. Here placed on rotten ships anchored in the bay or crowded into sugar warehouses they died among horrors not to be told.

The Last Campaign.—While Arnold escaped punishment, West Point and the Hudson did not fall into English hands. The next year six thousand Frenchmen, who had landed in Rhode Island, crossed the river and joined the forces of Washington. Clinton in New York city deceived by the movements of the American general diligently prepared for an expected attack. While he was busy, Washington with the French and American army was hurrying south to capture Cornwallis, who after devastating the States south had marched into Virginia. Before Clinton could reach Cornwallis at Yorktown with aid, that general had been forced to surrender. Washington now confident of final success led his troops back to the north, established his headquarters at Newburg on the Hudson, and waited for the declaration of peace.

CHAPTER XI.

In the year in which Cornwallis surrendered at Yorktown the thirteen States united under one general government. Each colony had early in the war formed a State government. During the Revolution, however, there was no common government except as each State sent delegates to congress at Philadelphia and allowed that body to do what was necessary to carry on the war.

The constitution adopted in 1781 was called the Articles of Confederation. It had been prepared the year after the Declaration of Independence, and ratified by New York the following year, but did not go into effect until adopted by Maryland, the thirteenth State. The confederated States were expected to act as one nation ; but there was no president, nothing but a congress which could advise the States what to do, but could not make them obey. The government was really a league of friendship between thirteen separate nations.

New York a Nation.—Accordingly within the limits of New York the laws of the State government were supreme. The power to levy taxes on goods brought from abroad, the control of the harbor of New York city, and the right to coin money,—powers now belonging to the United States government,—were then held by the legislature of the State. The State was generally ready to do what the common welfare demanded. New York has the distinction of being the only one of the thirteen States which, during the war, met every request of congress for men and money ; the State gave even more than was asked.

The Western Territory.—With like spirit New York took the lead of the States in giving up to congress its claims over the western territory. The United States at the close of the Revolution lay between the Atlantic ocean and the Mississippi river. This land was cut into two strips by the Alleganies ; to the east of the mountains were the thirteen States ; to the west was the territory which in colonial times belonged to the separate colonies. The land from which the States of Ohio and Indiana have since been marked out was claimed at the same time by New York and several other States. The difficulty was completely solved by all giving up the control of the territory to congress.

Revenue Taxes.—While New York was liberal in the matter of war supplies and its western lands, it was selfish in taking all the duties from foreign trade. If the general congress was to have any power at all it was necessary that it should levy and collect these duties. This privilege the State had voted to congress while the English were still in the city ; but when the English were gone and the revenues increased, the legislature took back the gift and refused congress any control of the harbor of New York city. Meanwhile the State had been making treaties with the Indian tribes just as an independent nation would do. This was before the continental army was disbanded.

Evacuation.—For two years after the victory at Yorktown, Washington waited at Newburg for the treaty of peace. His ill-paid army which was still needed to watch the English in New York city complained bitterly of the treatment of congress and was even ready to make Washington king. At last on the twenty-fifth of November, a day ever since known in the city as evacuation day. the army of America marched down the Bowery road as the last English ship sailed away.

It was a sorry sight which met the patriot eyes, as many of them after seven years of banishment looked for their homes. The city

had greatly changed. Shortly after the English captured the town
,a raging fire had wiped out nearly one-third of the city ; houses
and churches had been used by the soldiers and horses.   One minister returned to find his church used for a stable, and was able to
gather together but thirty-seven of his two hundred church
members.

A few days later, December fourth, in Fraunces' tavern, Wash-

SCENE OF WASHINGTON'S FAREWELL.

ington took tearful leave of his fellow soldiers and was rowed across
the river to begin his homeward journey to Mount Vernon. As
the people who watched the boat move off turned from the scene,
they felt the full effect of the terrible conflict ; then with broken
families they began to rebuild their homes from the blackened
ruins.

Treatment of the Tories.—All their bitter hatred now fell
upon their neighbors who had favored the king. Many of the
tories did not dare to return ; and most of those who showed themselves were forced by persecution to move away. A mass meeting
of the citizens of the interior was held at Fort Plain ; and soon after
New York city was evacuated, an old time gathering of the Sons of

Liberty was held in the Fields. At these meetings passionate speakers stirred up the hatred of the people against the tories. As a result the legislature passed a law banishing those who had supported the king. This law was contrary to the treaty of peace with England; it was unjust too, in the minds of such men as Hamilton and Schuyler; and by the efforts of these men the law was finally repealed.

Albany and the West.—The English, also, broke the treaty by refusing to give up the forts at Oswego, Ogdensburg and Niagara. One effect of this was to keep away from Albany the fur trade which had made it the lively city of colonial days. At the close of the Revolution, Albany had three thousand inhabitants, and was the sixth city in size in the United States; it continued to prosper; for the increased grain crops on all sides, especially to the north and west, made it for some years the grain centre of America.

To the westward the settlers were now pouring in a flood. The Iroquois who had made war against their old friends the colonists were doomed to lose their kingdom in central New York. To the northward the settlements which were begun before the Revolution were revived; Clinton county was settled and received the name of the governor. Many of the settlers in all parts of the State were soldiers to whom land was given in return for their services. Among them, General Steuben, a volunteer from Germany, was rewarded with sixteen thousand acres in Oneida county.

New England Settlers.—The immigrants to central New York were largely from Massachusetts and Connecticut. The original charters of those colonies were so worded as to give them some claim to the western part of New York. The claims of Massachusetts were settled by giving to residents of that State a right to occupy millions of acres in the Genesee valley, along Seneca lake and between the Oswego and Chenango rivers. Thus these regions were largely settled by people from the less fertile farms of New England.

Hugh White, from Connecticut, made an advance settlement at Whitestown, near the present Utica, and from thence a wagon road was made later through to the Genesee, thus opening to settlement the third great river valley of New York State.

The Population of the State at this time was a little over a quarter of a million, or one-twentieth of the population of 1880, a hundred years later. The population of 250,000 which New York had in 1780 was less than the number of people who in 1880 lived in the city of Buffalo; but ten years after the Revolution Buffalo was simply a storehouse, built for the fur trade at the foot of Lake Erie.

In New York city there were twenty-five thousand people; the place then occupied but a small fraction of its present limits. The city quickly revived after the English left; the next year congress, which had been meeting at Philadelphia, removed thither, and at the same time the State legislature, after trying Poughkeepsie, Kingston and Albany as State capitals came to New York city and there remained for four years. During all those years George Clinton was governor of the State, being elected at the end of each term of three years almost without opposition.

The Board of Regents.—One of the first acts of the legislature after assembling at New York city was to create a Board of Regents to take charge of King's college. This school was closed when the English occupied the city, but it was revived under the name of Columbia college and its first graduate thereafter was the governor's nephew, DeWitt Clinton. All higher schools and colleges of the State were afterward put in charge of the Board of Regents; but the common free schools were as yet hardly thought of.

Weakness of the Confederacy.—While the State prospered and its government grew strong, the government of the thirteen

States was fast proving a failure. Washington was freely pointing out the weakness of the league of States ; Hamilton was calling for a stronger government. Congress was despised; it was no longer the able body which made the Declaration of Independence. The great men of New York and of other States preferred to be elected to the State legislatures where their votes would count for something.

Although the State treasuries were filling up, congress could hardly pay its debts. It made one last appeal to the States for the revenues of the ports ; all agreed, except New York which refused to give up its fast increasing profits. The condition of things was becoming desperate. England was looking gleefully at the apparent failure of the United States.

A New Constitution.—A convention of delegates from the States was finally called to meet at Philadelphia, in 1787, to revise the Articles of Confederation. The convention soon found that they must write an entirely new constitution. To this, Governor Clinton of New York and a majority of the legislature were opposed. They were unwilling to give up any of the sovereign rights of the State. When two of the three delegates from New York, Yates and Lansing, found that the Philadelphia convention was bent upon making a new constitution, they left the meeting and went home, leaving Alexander Hamilton to represent the State alone.

From May till September the convention labored on, and after much strife agreed upon the present constitution of the United States. Then came the struggle for its adoption in the different States.

The Two Parties.—While one State and another were agreeing to the constitution, the opposition in New York was bitter. It was with difficulty that a convention could even be called to consider the question ; such a meeting of delegates elected from the different counties was called, however, to meet at Poughkeepsie in 1788, with power to adopt or reject the new constitution.   The opposition were in a clear majority and Governor Clinton was elected president of the meeting.

Joined with Clinton in opposing the new union were Yates, Lansing and Melancthon Smith.   They and their party were known as anti-federalists.   They believed in State rights; they argued that the proposed government would have too much power and would result in the president's becoming king.   They appealed strongly to the selfishness of the people of New York by showing that the wealth now pouring into the State treasury at New York city would go to all the States alike.

On the other side were Alexander Hamilton, Philip Schuyler, John Jay and Robert R. Livingston.   These men and those of the same mind were known as the federalist party.   They argued that the confederacy was a failure, and that a more perfect union was a necessity; that such a union would bring so many benefits that the State could well afford to give up some of its revenue.   These arguments together with a full explanation of the proposed constitution were fully circulated among the people of America in the famous papers of Hamilton known as the Federalist.   These articles, published in New York city papers, were largely the means of converting the voters of the State to believe in the new union.

Adoption.—But events moved the convention at Poughkeepsie more than arguments.   While the representatives of New York were debating, New Hampshire, the ninth State, ratified; and since it had been agreed that when nine States ratified the constitution, it should go into effect among them, the union was assured.   Then Virginia, the most populous State, after hesitating, came in as the tenth State.

As still day after day the men of New York held back, Hamilton in a three hours' speech at Poughkeepsie again argued eloquently for adoption. Tears were seen in the eyes of listeners ; the opposition wavered, and enough came over to the side of the federalists so that on the final vote of fifty-seven delegates, a bare majority of three brought New York into the union.

Beginning of the New Union.—The deed once done seemed to the reluctant people the best thing to be done, and the friends of the new government rapidly came to be a majority. All felt the more secure because Washington would surely be made president. All strife in the State was not over, and owing to quarrels of the two parties no electors were chosen and so New York had no part in the first election of Washington. Egbert Benson and four others were elected as the first members of the house of representatives from the State, and after a time the legislature selected Rufus King and Philip Schuyler to be the first United States senators.

The fourth of March, 1789, the day set for the beginning of the new government, was greeted at New York city, where the old congress had met and where the new congress was to assemble, with the firing of cannon. The new order of things started slowly ; and it was April thirtieth when Washington was ready to be inaugurated. In his triumphal march from Mount Vernon he had come over the bay as he had departed five years before. The new president, standing in Federal hall, Wall street, received the oath of office from Robert R. Livingston.

The inauguration day was joyous with processions and banquets, solemn with services in the churches, and brilliant at its close with fireworks and illuminations. Such scenes there were as well might be commemorated, a hundred years later, April 30th, 1889, with a glorious celebration. With such ceremonies New York yielded up the sovereign power which it had held for fourteen years and became an inseparable part of the American republic.

SUMMARY OF EVENTS,—PERIOD III.

1775.   Temporary State government established.
Capture of Ticonderoga ; expedition to northern New York and Canada.

1776.   Capture of New York city by the English.
New York ratifies the Declaration of Independence.

1777.   Burgoyne's expedition ; battle of Oriskany ; battles of Saratoga ; surrender of Burgoyne.
State constitution adopted ; Clinton governor.

1778.   Cherry Valley massacre.

1779.   Sullivan's expedition ; Wayne's capture of Stony Point.

1780.   Arnold's treason at West Point.

1781.   Washington's army leave New York for the last campaign at Yorktown.
Articles of Confederation take effect.

1783.   Evacuation of New York city.

1784.   Board of Regents formed.
The legislature and congress meet at New York city.

1787.   Formation of the constitution of the United States.

1788.   New York adopts the constitution.

1789.   Inauguration of Washington at New York city.

PERIOD IV.

CHAPTER XII.

In the Last Decade of the Eighteenth Century.— 1790–1800.

New York city in 1789 and 1790 was a lively place; it had recovered from the effects of the war; it was the capital of the State and of the United States. Its citizens were among the leaders of the new government. Alexander Hamilton, as the secretary of the treasury, was the foremost man of Washington's administration; his plans for a national revenue put the government on a sound foundation. In order to get a majority of congress to support his measures he had to agree with Jefferson, of Virginia, to fix the permanent capital of the nation on the Potomac river. When this was decided, congress, after being at New York city for a little over a year, adjourned to Philadelphia, there to remain until the new city of Washington was ready. The removal of the capital was no loss to the business interests of New York city.

Parties and Politics.—About the two men, Hamilton and Jefferson, the people of the nation were gathering into two parties. The party of Hamilton, who kept the name of federalists, were for so enforcing the constitution as to make a strong national government. Among the men of this party in New York State, were John Jay, then chief justice of the United States, and Schuyler and King, the United States senators.

(118)

The followers of Jefferson, most of whom had been anti-federalists, took the name of republicans. They were suspicious of the new constitution and still fearful of a return to a monarchy. In New York the republicans were led by the governor, George Clinton, and by Aaron Burr. This Burr was a young and able man ; he was rapidly growing in popular favor, and after Schuyler's short term of two years he took his place in the senate of the United States. Clinton had in 1792 been for fifteen years governor of the State. In that year the federalists endeavored to defeat him and took John Jay for their candidate. In a vote of 16,000,* Clinton was declared elected by a majority of one hundred and eight, after throwing out the votes of three federalist counties on account of some mistake in reporting the returns. There was a contest at once; the State was in a turmoil ; party spirit ran high. Jay. who had a plain majority of the votes, submitted calmly to the decision, and Clinton took the office for another term of three years.

In the same year Washington and Adams were reëlected for their second terms. Adams was not chosen vice-president without opposition ; for George Clinton received fifty of the one hundred and thirty-two electoral votes.

John Jay Governor.—At the following election for governor, in 1795, the federalist party again nominated John Jay, as if to test the decision of three years before. George Clinton wisely refused to be a candidate and Jay was elected by a large majority. At the time of his election, Jay was coming from England, where he had just made the famous treaty, known as the Jay treaty, by which America gave up much in order to keep peace with England. While time has shown that such a course was best, Jay's action was then bitterly denounced. Hamilton, attempting to

---

* The vote was, Clinton 8,440; Jay, 8,332. This vote of 16,772 was but five per cent of the population. At the present time fifteen to twenty per cent of the population vote at the election of governor. This shows how few men were voters when there was a property qualification.

address a meeting in Wall street in favor of the treaty, was pelted with stones. At this time the Livingston family, among them Brockholst, the brother-in-law of Jay, joined the growing party of republicans.

Still the federalist party was strong enough in the State to control the legislature the next year and thus to choose electors who voted for John Adams to succeed Washington as president. At that time and for many years afterward the legislature selected the electors of president, so that there was no presidential election by the voters of the State.

The Case of Vermont.—While national matters were taking so much attention, the State had important questions to decide. Soon after the formation of the union, the long-continued Vermont trouble was settled. It had broken out more than once since the days of Allen and Warner; the right of New York over the land between the Connecticut river and Lake Champlain had never been enforced. During the Revolution, Vermont had declared itself independent of New York under the name of New Connecticut. So matters went along until after the constitution was adopted, when New York consented to Vermont's coming in as a separate State. Thus the long struggle was ended, and Vermont had the honor of being the first member of the union received after the original States.

Counties.—There was quite enough territory left in the State to busy the law-makers. Vast tracts in the central and western parts were sold to speculators. At one time five and a half million acres of State land were sold either fraudulently or foolishly at an average price of twenty cents an acre. New counties were fast being formed. For nearly a hundred years after the organization of the original ten counties, there was no change in the number. A few years before the Revolution two counties, now called Montgomery and Washington, were set off. No further division of the State was made until about 1790 when Clinton county in the north, Ontario in the west, and Columbia and Rensselaer counties east of the Hudson were formed. About the same time, parts of Montgomery, formerly Tryon county, once so overrun by the Indians, were laid out as Herkimer, Otsego, Saratoga and Schoharie counties, and along the Pennsylvania border Tioga was the first county established.

Just before the close of the century a number of interior counties with Indian names, Cayuga, Chenango, Delaware, Oneida and Onondaga, were formed by the legislature. Steuben then marked the limit of settlement along the southern tier; Essex was laid out by the side of its northern neighbor, Clinton, and from the large original counties along the west bank of the Hudson Rockland and Greene were set off. Thus the number of counties at the beginning of the nineteenth century had increased to thirty.

Water Ways.—It is noticeable that counties lying along water ways were first settled ; that the western lands of Ontario county were taken up before the central territory of Cortland county. The net-work.of lakes and rivers which covered the State rendered its settlement rapid. The 300,000 inhabitants of 1790 had become almost 600,000 ten years later. The people had already taken up the best farms along the upper Mohawk, the Genesee and Lake Champlain.

Many plans were proposed for improving the navigation of rivers and for cutting canals. Even before the Revolution the importance of connecting the waters of the Hudson river with Lake Champlain and with Lake Erie or Lake Ontario had been seen. In 1792 two companies were formed to make the Mohawk river navigable by cutting canals around the impassable places. Four years later a private company dug a canal three miles long around Little Falls, and made shorter cuts at German Flats, and from the head waters of the Mohawk to Wood creek, which flows into Oneida lake. But the canals were poor and costly ; along the rivers boats had to be moved against the stream by sails and poles ; so that wagons were still used largely in the central parts of the State to get produce and goods to and from Albany.

Roads and Mails.—The country roads were for the most part mere wagon tracks over roots and trees and through mud-holes; bridges were almost unknown. The road from Whitestown through Geneva was before 1800 continued to Buffalo. To the northward another road led from Albany to Clinton county, along the old Indian trail to Canada. A post rider in these days took the mails once in two weeks from Albany to the Genesee valley.

Few letters were written in those days of few mails, no envelopes, no stamps, high postage and costly paper. The New York city post-office was in part of a private house and a few boxes were enough for the city of fifty thousand inhabitants. There were but four newspapers in the city a dozen years after the close of the Revolution, three at Albany, and outside of these places not more than ten newspapers were published in the State.

The City of New York was now growing faster than any other city in America. A writer of the time says, "The houses are generally built of brick and the roofs tiled; there remain a few houses after the old Dutch manner, but the English taste has prevailed almost a century. The principal part of the city lies on the east side of the island, although the buildings extend from one river to the other. The length of the city on the east side is about two miles, but falls much short of that distance on the banks of the Hudson. Its breadth, on an average, is nearly three-fourths of a mile, and circumference may be four miles."

The water supply of the city was a problem; the wells in the lower part of the city gave bitter water; and lines of wagons carried better water in hogsheads from wells then in the upper part of the city,—places now called "down town." The fresh water pond, where Canal street now is, was still a considerable body of water, and there John Fitch was working with a curious boat which he hoped to move with steam. The lack of good water was charged as the cause of the frequent epidemics of yellow fever which visited the city, carrying off in one year over two thousand victims.

Along the Hudson River new life was infused by the growth of New York city and the development of the interior; Hudson and Troy, places unknown at the close of the war, were outstripping the older towns. Hudson was made a port of entry in 1795, and at one time rivaled New York city in the amount of its shipping. Troy which was not settled until 1789 had before the close of the century nearly a million dollars of taxable property. "Grain and lumber were the source of this wealth."

Just south of Troy, at Albany, the capital of the State was permanently fixed in 1797; and that city has since remained the centre of the political warfare for which the State of New York has ever been noted.

Progress.—The year 1800 saw the log cabins of the settlers along the south banks of the St. Lawrence, along the river banks of the Pennsylvania border, while Elmira, Bath and Canandaigua were little huddles of houses which had just been left behind by the advance guard of settlers. By 1800 New York had passed from the fifth to the third in population and wealth among the States of the union.

The laboring men were still for the most part farmers; but they were beginning to find other work. Iron had been discovered in the State and was being mined and made up into various forms; the tanning of leather and the manufacture of clocks and hats were then infant industries. Among cloths, woolen, linen and even silk were made.

The Schools of the State, in the rush of this rapid progress, fared poorly. The first college organized by the Board of Regents was Union college, at Schenectady, in 1795. The next year the Regents reported fourteen academies under their charge. One of these schools was founded by Samuel Kirkland, the missionary to the Oneidas, a school which has grown into Hamilton college.

The year 1795 is to be remembered as the time of the beginning of schools far more important than colleges and academies; the common public schools of New York date from that time. The legislature then voted the sum of fifty thousand dollars yearly for five years for the schools of the State; and an equal amount was raised by the local taxation of the counties which chose to share in the distribution of the State money. Thus a hundred thousand dollars was spent on the common schools, the yearly cost of which a century later is twenty millions of dollars.

Slavery.—A fact which agrees well with the little attention paid to schools is that human slavery still existed in New York. There were at this time about twenty thousand negro slaves in the State, or one in every twenty-five or thirty of the people. This ratio was not so large as in early colonial times; the climate of New York did not foster slavery as did that of the southern States. John Jay had tried without success to prohibit slavery in the first constitution of the State; and as governor he renewed his efforts. When he was a candidate for reëlection in 1798, his opposition to slavery was used as an argument against him. But he was successful at the election and the next year partly successful in his efforts against slavery, and secured a law for the gradual freeing of the negroes.

The Council of Appointment.—Governor Jay found himself hampered by a council of four senators elected by the assembly to act with the governor in appointing officers. The governor thought that the senators should merely advise him; the council held that they with the governor had the actual power to appoint, and that a majority of the five, that is any three, could act even in opposition to the governor. This view of the matter was taken by a State convention called to settle the question. The number of appointed officers was large under the first constitution; such officers as mayors of cities, sheriffs of counties and justices of the peace were then ap-

pointed by the governor and his council. Not even the veto power
was given to the governor under the first constitution, but it was
vested in another council, called the council of revision.

The Trouble with France.—State politics now gave way to
the excitement caused by the threatened war with France. When,
a few years before, Genet (zhch'nä) came from France to excite sympathy for his country, he was heartily received by the republicans
of New York and married a daughter of George Clinton. But in
1798 there was less sympathy for the French government which so
basely insulted the United States. It was decided to fortify New
York city, which had fallen an easy prey to the English army, at a
cost of over a million dollars ; and Hamilton was under the aged
Washington to be the real leader of the army. But the army never
was needed ; and the mistakes of President Adams in dealing with
the trouble with France helped to bring about the defeat of the
federalist party at the next national election.

Defeat of the Federalists.—The year 1800 marks the downfall
of the federalist party. The death of Washington and the ill-feeling between the federalist leaders, Hamilton and Adams, hastened
the defeat. New York, as has happened so often since. was the
State which decided the presidential election. When the legislature chose electors favorable to Jefferson, the defeat of Adams was
certain.

The next year John Jay refused to be again a candidate for governor ; and George Clinton, after six years of private life, was
elected for a seventh term governor of the State of New York.

CHAPTER XIII.

PARTY STRIFE AND NATIONAL WAR.—1801–1815.

When in the opening year of the century George Clinton again became governor, he at once discharged all office-holders not of his party. This was the beginning of the spoils system in the politics of New York. Jay refused to remove competent officers, whom Clinton had left in office; but henceforth party allegiance rather than ability was to be the first test of the public service.

Leaders and Factions.—The republican party was now in full control of the State. Among the

GEORGE CLINTON.

party leaders were Aaron Burr, Robert R. Livingston and DeWitt Clinton. Burr had reached the high office of vice-president of the United States; but he was looked upon with distrust; since he had been willing that a defect in the constitution should give him the presidency, an office to which the people had elected Thomas Jefferson. Chancellor * Robert R. Livingston was appointed minister to France by President Jefferson and there negotiated the purchase of Louisiana. Another distinguished citizen of New York had represented the nation at the court of France, Gouverneur Morris. Just before the federalist

---

* The chancellor was the chief judge of the court of chancery, an officer not named in the present constitution of the State.

party lost control of the legislature, Morris was elected to the United States senate.

The man destined to be the most notable of the leaders of the time was DeWitt Clinton. As his uncle had led New York for a quarter of a century, so he was to be a leader in the State during the first twenty-five years of the nineteenth century. He began public life as the secretary of George Clinton ; in 1802 he was elected to the United States senate, but soon resigned to accept an appointment as mayor of New York city, a place at that time of more political power.

The methods of politicians were less criticised then than they are now. Members of the legislature voted charters for banks and in return openly received stock at special prices. Party strife was bitter and called forth personal hatred. The powerful republican party was soon split into factions, one known as Burrites and the other as the Clinton and Livingston faction. Burr, though strong in the State, received a national rebuke for his readiness to be made president in 1800 by being left off the ticket when Jefferson was reëlected in 1804. In his place George Clinton was chosen vice-president.* Burr, smarting under this treatment, turned to his State for vindication and announced himself as an independent candidate for governor to succeed Clinton. He was supported largely by the federalists, but failed to get all their votes on account of the opposition of Hamilton. As a result Burr was defeated and the regular republican candidate, Morgan Lewis, was elected.

Hamilton and Burr.—Burr now turned his hatred upon Hamilton and easily made an excuse to challenge him to a duel. Dueling, then so popular in the southern States, was tolerated in New York. DeWitt Clinton had fought a duel ; Brockholst Livingston

---

* George Clinton was vice-president from 1801 to 1812, dying in office in that year at the age of seventy-three.

had killed a man on Manhattan island ; and a son of Hamilton had in a like combat been fatally wounded.

Hamilton was goaded into accepting the challenge of Burr. One early July morning of 1804 the two met across the river from New York city on the New Jersey shore. That famous duel resulted in the death of the greatest statesman that New York has ever given to the union ; it forever blasted the hopes of an ambitious politician, and made dueling a crime.

Detested by the people, Burr fled from the State, boldly plotted treason against the government, lived an adventurous life in Europe, and finally returned to live in New York city to a soured and use-less old age.

Education.—Morgan Lewis, who defeated Aaron Burr and thus became the third governor of New York, was interested in schools. The appropriation of fifty thousand dollars a year ran out in 1800, and since then the legislature had tried to raise money for the schools by a lottery. In 1805, at the recommendation of Governor Lewis the proceeds of five hundred thousand acres of the State lands were set aside, the interest of which was forever to be used for the schools of the State. This was the beginning of the permanent school fund.

The State did not as yet provide any free public schools ; but at this time a free school society was formed in New York city by private subscription and State aid, to give an education to poor children. In 1809 the first free school building in New York city was completed : but it was a charity school : it was yet to be years before free schools were thrown open to all ; before the law-makers ceased to offer education as a charity to the poor, and began to realize that it is their first duty to provide an education for all.

General Advancement.—Several events in and about the year 1807 mark it as a time of awakening not only in education but in morals, literature and mechanical arts. Prisons began to be built with some thought of cleanliness and decency, from which criminals would come out better instead of worse; in New York city the first insane asylum was built, and public hospitals were erected. Doctors, by a law of the State, were required to show some fitness for their work, whereas before they had practiced medicine without a license.

In New York city there were eight daily papers; one of them, the Evening Post, began its life with the century; another the Commercial Advertiser, had once had for its editor Noah Webster, whose speller educated a generation of Americans and whose dictionary has instructed all English-speaking people. Washington Irving, the first master of American literature, was publishing the Salmagundi and making men laugh with his Knickerbocker's History of New York. An awakening interest in the history of the State was shown by the formation of the New York Historical society, an association which has in many ways added to the fame of New York. In 1809, this society modestly celebrated the two hundredth anniversary of Hudson's discovery.

In the history of manufactures a notable event was the building of cotton mills at Whitesboro and of a woolen mill at Oriskany, "believed now to be the oldest wool-making institution in the United States," where broadcloth worth twelve dollars a yard was made from wool costing a dollar and a quarter a pound.

The First Steamboat.—But the most remarkable event in the history of inventions which occurred within the bounds of the State was the running of the first successful steamboat. In 1807 the Clermont made the trip from New York city to Albany; the boat was made by Robert Fulton, encouraged and aided by Robert R. Livingston. On the seventh of August the rude craft lay at its dock ready to begin a journey against wind and tide; the uncovered paddle wheels began to turn and the boat moved away from the derisive crowd which lined the shore of the Hudson. On it went through the Palisades, making one frightened farmer think that he had seen " the devil on his way to Albany in a saw-mill "; and after a triumphant trip of thirty-two hours it steamed up to the Albany wharf.

Fulton did not invent the steamboat; John Fitch and others had moved boats by the use of steam power; but Fulton was the first man to make a paying steamboat. At that time sail boats made the trip between Albany and New York city in from two to five days, according to the wind; and the charge for such a trip including board was from six to ten dollars. The Clermont became a regular passenger boat; improvements in steam navigation followed, until thirty years later steamboats crossed the ocean.

The Embargo.—The improved navigation of the Hudson river made the need of a water way to the interior more keenly felt. The State was urged to build canals. The legislature ordered the Mohawk route surveyed; but before it was ready to act, threatened war with England prevented all thought of interior improvement.

When England and France in their quarrel with each other shut out our ships from their ports, our government, hoping to force them to terms, decreed an embargo. The embargo forbade foreign ships from entering our harbors and prevented any ship from sailing to a foreign port. At that time New York city had in its foreign trade fairly outstripped its rivals, Boston and Philadelphia, and was the commercial centre of the continent. The State by means of its commerce and agriculture had taken second rank in population among the States of the union. But the embargo fell like a blight. The business of New York city was at a standstill; ships rotted at the docks; warehouses and stores were closed; farmers found no market for their produce.

A Change in Governor and in President.—The embargo was laid in the last months of 1807; during the same year an election

for governor occurred.   After the scattering of the Burrites, the
 republican party, or the demo-
crats, as they now began to be
called, again split into factions.
DeWitt Clinton and his followers
had quarreled with the Livingstons and Governor Lewis; Clinton after looking about for a
candidate to oppose Lewis selected a young judge, Daniel D.
Tompkins, and succeeded in electing him.   For himself DeWitt
Clinton had the presidency in
view, as the next year, 1808,
would bring the fifth presidential
election.   As Jefferson was to re-
tire, it was argued with some
show of reason that the president,

DANIEL D. TOMPKINS.

who at four elections had come from Virginia, should be taken from
New York.   The democratic party, however, selected Madison of
Virginia as its candidate, and New York had to be content with
the reëlection of George Clinton to the vice-presidency.

The War Question.—President Madison took office in a stormy
time.   War with England was at hand.   The embargo had been
raised on the retirement of Jefferson in the spring of 1809; it had
been a disastrous experiment and had not hindered the English in
their attempts to ruin our commerce; war seemed to many to be
the only recourse.   To this a majority of the people of New York
and New England were opposed; for a war would fall most heavily
upon those commercial States.   The opposition to a war revived for
a while the federalist party at the north; and in New York, for
the first time in ten years, they controlled the legislature and the

council of appointment. They replaced democratic officers with federalists, only to have them swept from office when the next election brought the usual democratic success.

The war party was increasing fast, for the acts of England were becoming more and more unbearable; the English searched our vessels, imprisoned our seamen, held the western forts which at the peace of 1783 they had agreed to give up, and incited the Indians to slaughter. Still President Madison strove for peace and only when persuaded that his reëlection in 1812 depended on favoring war with England did he join the war party. The federalist party had no candidate for the presidency; but the opponents of Madison supported DeWitt Clinton of New York and though they carried seven States, failed to elect him.

The War of 1812.—Before the presidential election of 1812, however, the war had actually begun. In this war New York from her position was a most important State, but it was not so much exposed as in the war of the Revolution. The conflict raged more to the westward; and while the border line of the State was longer than in the first war with England, yet no incursions of the enemy pierced the interior; no valleys suffered from the Indian's fire and scalping knife; and above all New York city did not fall into the hands of the enemy.

Along the Border.—At the extreme west of the State, the Niagara river separates but narrowly the two countries; and here along a line of thirty miles the battles raged for three years. From Buffalo and Black Rock northward through Lewiston to Fort Niagara on Lake Ontario, the Americans held a line of defences, while across the river the English fortified Fort Erie opposite Buffalo and strengthened their border through Queenstown to Fort George.

Back and forth over the Niagara river the two armies crossed and recrossed. On the Canadian side of the stream our armies gained

great glory but little advantage at the
battles of Queenstown Heights and of
Lundy's Lane ; they made little headway into Canada. On the other hand
western New York was in danger of
the enemy. The little villages of Buffalo and Black Rock and others along
the border of Lake Ontario were burned
by the English aided by a small rem-
nant of the Iroquois. At last the capture of Forts Erie and George by the
Americans, the victory of Perry on
Lake Erie and the success of General
Harrison about Detroit freed the western part of New York from
danger.

The border of the State
along Lake Ontario and the
St. Lawrence suffered
much. Sackett's Harbor
was the most important
point and the centre of
supplies ; here the heroism
of a few brave defenders
twice held the place against
the British fleet. Oswego
and Ogdensburg, less fortunate, were sacked.
In return our
armies captured
York, now Toron-
to, gained some

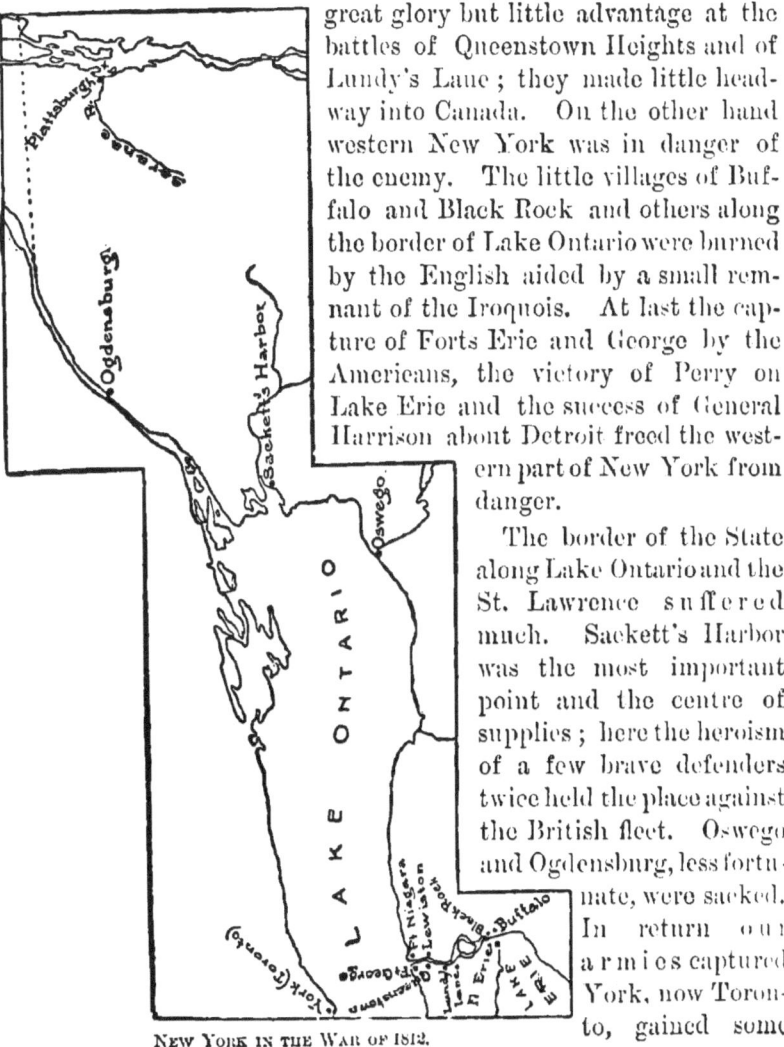

NEW YORK IN THE WAR OF 1812.

successes on the north bank of the St. Lawrence, but did not get far into Canada.

On Lake Ontario the English ships at first held undisputed sway ; then along the shore the Americans rapidly built vessels ; they dragged the iron works laboriously overland from Albany ; and soon they made the lake the scene of stirring events such as fill the pages of romance.

At New York City.—From these inland scenes of warfare, New York city was distant a long journey of two or three weeks. Since the war of 1812 was largely a naval contest, fought out on different parts of the Atlantic, the port of New York was a centre of supplies for the American navy. Hither such famous ships as the Constitution, Wasp, and Essex returned from victories which shattered the world-feared navy of Great Britain, until finally the English fleet lay off Sandy Hook and blockaded the harbor.

When the news of the capture and burning of Washington was received, New York city expected the long looked for attack. The city was poorly protected ; but money was voted for fortifications ; and better than that everybody turned out to throw up earth ; schools took a holiday ; printers omitted a paper, in order that all, men and boys, might help on the work. Soon the Narrows, Brooklyn, Harlem Heights and the islands in the river bristled with forts, whose strength the enemy never tested.

On Lake Champlain.—Although the English did not attack the forts at the mouth of the Hudson, they did not overlook the importance of the Champlain and the Hudson valleys. Fourteen thousand veterans, trained in the wars with Napoleon, started from Canada over the route made famous by Burgoyne. But this army never reached the upper waters of the lake. At Plattsburgh a small army of Americans stood at the Saranac river to oppose the land force of the invaders. On the lake Commodore Macdonough (mak-don'-oh) gathered together a few boats to meet the English squadron rounding Cumberland head. In one of the pluckiest fights of that war Macdonough scattered the ships of the English ; the spirit of victory electrified the small band on the shore ; and the veterans of Europe fled back to the Canadian lines.

By this time the anti-war party in New York State had about disappeared ; but all were glad to hear, in the first days of 1815, that peace had been made with England. The treaty did not promise that for which the war had been fought ; but the English navy had learned to fear the war ships of America ; and never again were the merchant vessels sailing from New York city boarded by English officers in times of peace. New York had at fearful cost done her part with the other seventeen States in upholding our national honor.

Schools.—During the second war with England the legislature created the office of superintendent of common schools, thus giving the slowly forming school system a head. Gideon Hawley was the first superintendent of schools and he served for a salary of three hundred dollars.

The West Point military academy was organized by the United States government at the beginning of the war. This famous school grew out of a military encampment at that Revolutionary point, and provided for a trained and educated soldiery.

A fund for the three colleges of the State, Columbia, Union and Hamilton, and for other worthy objects was raised at this time by the unworthy means of a lottery, a scheme of money-getting which people were just beginning to criticise.

It was during the war of 1812 that a few devout men and women of New York city began to gather children in churches and in private houses on Sunday to teach them. Many good people shook their heads at this idea of breaking the holy day. Such people would have been very slow to believe that before the century closed over a million* people would be attending the Sunday schools of the State, and that next to the Christian church the Sunday school would exert the greatest power for good.

---

* The figures as given by the State Sunday School Association, June, 1890, are,—teachers and officers, 114,460: children, 769,985; adults, 184,832; total, 1,069,277; number of schools, 7,594.

CHAPTER XIV.

THE ERIE CANAL.—1816-1825.

Clintonians and Bucktails.—For a number of years after the war of 1812 political parties in New York were not divided on national questions; the contests were largely for the offices. De-Witt Clinton was still influential; but his enemies were numerous; and whereas they had once gathered under the lead of Burr and later under that of Livingston, they now followed Governor Tompkins. Tompkins was three times reëlected to the office which he first received in 1807, and meanwhile had become the bitter political enemy of his early friend, DeWitt Clinton. The governor filled his office with credit during the war and began to be spoken of for the presidency. One of his leading supporters was the young and ambitious Martin Van Buren.

Another ally of the governor was the society of Tammany. This organization, which took the name of a celebrated Indian chief, was begun at the time of Washington's inauguration as a social club. Later on it became a political society and often controlled the city of New York, the government of the State, and even national affairs. Tammany was always arrayed against DeWitt Clinton, and in 1812 helped to defeat him for the presidency.

Clinton's faction of the democratic party included most of the old federalists and they were known as the Clintonians. The common name of the opposition party was bucktails, a name given them after some of the Tammany men once appeared with deer's tails in their hats.

(137)

The Elections of 1816 and 1817.—Tompkins' fourth election as governor was in 1816, the year of the seventh presidential election. When on the fourth of the next March, Madison should finish his second term, the office of president would have been held by Virginians for twenty-four out of the twenty-eight years. The northern people, especially those of New York, felt that they had a claim on the presidency, and talked about the "Virginia dynasty." The congressmen of the southern States, however, succeeded in nominating Monroe, of Virginia. At that time political conventions for nominating party candidates were unknown and such nominations were made by the party's congressmen or by the State legislators.

Virginia and New York were rival States. Virginia had led in population from early colonial days; but since 1776 New York had passed from the fifth to the second place among the States and it was probable that the census of 1820 would show that it had left Virginia behind.

To compromise matters the office of vice-president was given to Governor Tompkins; and so a few days before the fourth of March, 1817, he resigned the governorship which he had ably held for ten years. According to the constitution then, the lieutenant-governor did not fill out the term; but a new election was held at which De-Witt Clinton was almost unanimously chosen.

Abolition of Slavery.—One of the last acts of Governor Tompkins' ten years' administration was his most illustrious deed. He advised and secured the passage of a law ordering the total abolition of slavery in New York on and after independence day of 1827. The gradual emancipation begun under Governor John Jay had reduced the number of slaves one-half; yet ten thousand human beings still remained in servitude within the State; but the dis-grace was to be forever wiped out ten years afterward on the fourth of July, 1827. For this act of justice the State is also largely indebted to the society of friends, or Quakers of New York city, and to William Jay and Peter Jay, sons of the former governor.

The Erie Canal.—Independence day of the year 1817 is also a notable time in the history of the State. On that day in the town of Rome, Oneida county, the first spadeful of earth was thrown up in the digging of the Erie canal. The Erie canal has a history.

Before Hudson discovered the bay, the Iroquois had seen the advantages of New York for internal navigation. The great lakes, Lake Champlain, and the many little lakes stretching north and south, with the St. Lawrence, Hudson, Mohawk, Genesee and Susquehanna rivers make a wonderful collection of water routes. To the Indians the great harbor was nothing; to the first white men the interior water ways were of little account. Then as the Indians left the centre of the State and the white men entered, connection between the salt and fresh waters was demanded.

The Makers of the Canal.—Who first thought of a canal cannot be told. In 1724, a hundred years before the Erie canal was completed, Cadwallader Colden foresaw such a "scene of inland navigation as cannot be paralleled in any other part of the world." Various suggestions, for the most part to deepen and to widen the rivers, were made just before the Revolution.

Washington was interested in a project to connect the Atlantic with the great lakes; he suggested a canal from Lake Erie to the Potomac river and Chesapeake bay. While the army was encamped at Newburg, he ascended the Mohawk with George Clinton to determine whether inland navigation to Lake Ontario were possible.

The first man to put in definite shape these various projects was Gouverneur Morris; he advised what yet may be realized,—a ship canal. About the time of Washington's administration the project of a canal seemed to be abandoned for a plan to make the Mohawk river navigable. But the short canals around Little Falls, at German Flats and from the Mohawk to Wood creek were costly failures.

The project still lacked a man to put life in it, a man to give time and energy, to argue and to labor, to persuade legislators and farmers, to risk popularity and scorn fortune, a great man and one ready to give his greatness to the success of a life's work. Such a man was DeWitt Clinton; to him New York owes the Erie canal. As member of the legislature and as mayor of New York city during the first decade of the century he gave the best of his exertions to persuade the State to undertake the work.

DeWitt Clinton.

The First Step.—In 1808 the route of the canal was surveyed by Joseph Geddes, who dug the first salt well in Onondaga county. To the joy of the friends of a canal the project was reported practicable. Two years later the legislature appointed a committee to go over the route and reckon the cost; of this committee Gouverneur Morris and DeWitt Clinton were members, and Robert R. Livingston and Robert Fulton were afterward added; they decided against the plan of a canal to Lake Ontario, with a short canal around Niagara Falls; and they estimated the expense of the route direct to Lake Erie at five million dollars.

As the canal would be of great value to the western States, the United States government was asked to bear the expense; but fortunately congress did not bring the canal into national politics, but left it to New York's unaided energy. The approaching war of 1812, while it put a stop to all efforts for a canal, yet made its necessity still more clear. At one time cannon were dragged to Lake Ontario at an expense equal to twice their original cost.

Opposition.—At the close of the war DeWitt Clinton and others again went to work to combat the inaction of the legislature and the prejudice of the people. Objections were many. It was a wild scheme; it could never be done; it would bankrupt the State; the southern counties would pay for what would not benefit them.

At one time a friend of the canal found a company of German farmers along the very route who opposed the attempt. They could not understand about the locks; " Water cannot run up hill," said they. Finally to convince them the man dug a small ditch, made a lock of shingles, poured in a pailful of water and locked a chip up his little canal.

In 1817 the friends of the measure triumphed over all obstacles, obtained from the legislature a favorable vote, and in the same year began the work. Two years of well directed labor completed the canal from Rome to Utica. There were still many who were determined that the canal should go no farther; and they carried their opposition to the polls in the same year, 1819, when Governor Clinton's term was ended. There was an exciting contest for governor; Vice-President Tompkins threw his influence against the canal and accepted a nomination in opposition to DeWitt Clinton. There was a small majority for Clinton; but this majority meant that the work must go on and the canal be finished.

The Second Constitution.—Governor Clinton on beginning his second term advised the legislature to call a convention to frame a new constitution. The first State constitution, adopted in 1777, had carried the State government through two wars, and had been the fundamental law for nearly half a century; but its defects were many; and the need of something better was strongly felt. The convention was called and included among its members Daniel D.

Tompkins, then beginning his second term as vice-president; Martin Van Buren, who had just reached the United States senate in his rising career; Rufus King, the other senator, the last candidate of the federalist party for the presidency; Chancellor Kent * and Ambrose Spencer † of legal fame; and Stephen Van Rensselaer of the ancient family.

This convention spent two and a half months of the year 1821 at their work; and the next year the people voted to adopt the proposed constitution. This constitution as afterward amended did away with the property qualification of voters and gave the right to vote to all men except criminals and lunatics, except also negroes, who had to own two hundred and fifty dollars worth of property in order to vote.

The council of revision was abolished and the veto power given to the governor; the council of appointment was done away with; and the most of the town and county officers before appointed were made elective by the people. Circuit courts were established and the State divided into eight judicial districts. The assembly was fixed at one hundred and twenty-eight members and the senate at thirty-two; at which number they have since remained. At that time, however, there were eight senatorial districts, each district sending one senator each year for a term of four years. At the same time the term of the governor was shortened to two years; and the time of the State election was changed from April to the Tuesday following the first Monday of November. Accordingly for fifty years thereafter, the November of every even year was the time of the election of governor, and on the first of the succeeding January the governor was inaugurated.

---

* James Kent, author of Commentaries on American Law, was a celebrated jurist. He became chief justice of New York, his native State, in 1804, and a few years later was appointed chancellor.

† Ambrose Spencer was born in Connecticut; he was made chief justice of New York in 1810. Although a brother-in-law of DeWitt Clinton he was for a long time a political opponent.

The Rule of the Politicians.—In 1822, DeWitt Clinton, although he was still foremost in the building of the Erie canal, was growing more unpopular among the politicians ; so he decided not to be a candidate for reëlection.   He left the gubernatorial chair to Joseph C. Yates of Schenectady, and gave his time to the completion of the canal.

The politicians were supreme.   The year before, they removed from office Gideon Hawley, who for eight years had been the able superintendent of common schools.   They put in his place a young lawyer of so little ability, that to cover the blunder the legislature did away with the office and put the common schools under the secretary of state.

While this was the "era of good feeling" of Monroe's administration and the democrats were the only national party, it was in New York State a time of bitter personal rivalry.   The spoils system was there brought to perfection whence it was soon to be carried into the politics of the nation.   This controlling clique of politicians was known as the "Albany Regency" and was under the lead of Martin Van Buren and William L. Marcy.

In opposition to the arrogant rule of this political faction a party was growing up in the State under the name of the people's party. The leaders of this movement advocated the choosing of presidential electors by a vote of the people rather than by the legislature, and the nomination of party candidates by a convention of delegates rather than by members of the legislature.   This party in 1824 called the first State nominating convention ever held in New York to meet at Utica.

Before this convention met, in the last hours of the session of the legislature, the enemies of DeWitt Clinton rushed through a bill removing him from his office of canal commissioner.   Thus, as they thought, they would completely drive him from public sight. The people were amazed at the spiteful injustice done the man who had served as president of the canal commission faithfully and without pay; they held indignation meetings all over the State. When the people's party met at the Utica convention, they took up the popular cause, nominated Clinton for governor and triumphantly elected him.

The Canal Finished.—This election was a fitting event; De-Witt Clinton, in whose governorship the Erie canal was begun, thus came back into the high office in time to take charge of the completion of his life's work. As the summer of 1825 passed away, "Clinton's ditch," after eight years of building, lacked but a little of reaching from Albany to Buffalo.

The first cost of the work was seven million dollars, a fraction of the money expended in later years upon an unsatisfactory State capitol. A few years after its completion, the canal was enlarged; and this improvement together with mismanagement and stealing swelled the entire cost to over fifty million dollars or to almost eight times the original expense. The entire cost of the Erie canal has been more than repaid to the State.

The canal as finally enlarged is three hundred and sixty-three miles long and has seventy-two locks; its width is seventy feet, allowing boats of nearly twenty feet in width. Beginning at Albany it follows the Hudson to Cohoes, and thence part of the way to Schenectady it takes the north bank of the Mohawk; then it follows the windings of the Mohawk on its southern bank to Utica whence the long summit level of fifty miles reaches to Syracuse, leaving meanwhile the Mohawk at Rome. At Syracuse the Oswego canal connects with Lake Ontario; from Syracuse to Rochester many aqueducts are needed to take the canal over rivers and the Cayuga marshes. A few miles after crossing the Genesee, the longest level of the canal stretches out sixty-five miles to Lockport; where by five locks close together it rises to the thirty mile level which extends to Buffalo and Lake Erie.

For a third of the length the water is furnished by Lake Erie. The rest of the water comes from the Black river canal, Cazenovia lake and the reservoirs on the summit, all flowing toward Albany; so that the flow of the canal, except for a short distance, is from west to east.

The Celebration.—The water of Lake Erie entered the great ditch at Buffalo on the twenty-sixth day of October, 1825. A vast crowd of jubilant people were there; there were flags, cannon and gaily decked boats; DeWitt Clinton was there. The rushing in of the water was telegraphed to New York city. It was before Morse invented the telegraph; but it was done. Cannon had been placed at hearing distances along the towpath and the bank of the Hudson to New York city. It was an hour and a half from the time that the first cannon sounded on the shore of Lake Erie till the last gun echoed over New York bay.

From Buffalo a flotilla of brightly decorated canal boats began the first trip to the ocean. The "Seneca Chief" took the lead, carrying Governor Clinton and other noted men. One of the other boats was "Noah's Ark," with a cargo of eagles, bears, Indians and similar products of Ohio, Indiana and other States of the wild west. Everywhere along the canal, by day and by night, people were gathered to cheer the gay procession. Rochester joyfully welcomed the fleet at the great stone archway which carries the water over the Genesee. Albany was ablaze; and on the tenth day of the trip the ringing of bells and the noise of cannon told the people of New York city that the steamboats had towed the fleet to the mouth of the Hudson.

From the ships there in waiting came the challenge to the "Seneca Chief":—"Where are you from and what is your destination?" The reply came back, "From Lake Erie and bound for Sandy Hook."

A great number of crafts of all kinds then made out to sea, where DeWitt Clinton, taking up a keg of water from Lake Erie, poured it into the ocean, thus indicating the uniting of the great lakes with the Atlantic ocean. Then on the return of the boats to New York city the celebration continued ; processions, illuminations and fire-works formed a dazzling spectacle, worthy of doing honor to the greatest work of New York State.

Thus the year 1825 marks an era in the history of the State. It was just fifty years since the battle of Lexington and the flight of the English governor. For thirty-five years the nation had been established under the constitution. The fifteen counties into which the State was divided when Washington was inaugurated had increased to fifty-six, thus mapping out the State about as it was to remain. The population of the State which reached the first mil-lion during the war of 1812, was now half way toward another million. The census of 1820 had placed the State first in wealth and population. The building of the Erie canal gave New York a claim to be called then and thereafter the EMPIRE STATE.

SUMMARY OF EVENTS,—PERIOD IV.

1790.   The Vermont difficulty settled.
   Congress removed from New York city to Philadelphia.
1795.   John Jay governor.
1797.   Albany made the permanent capital.
1801.   George Clinton again governor.
1804.   Morgan Lewis governor.
   Killing of Hamilton by Burr.
1805.   The beginning of the school fund.
1807.   Daniel D. Tompkins governor.
   First trip of Fulton's steamboat.
   The embargo laid.

1812. Madison elected president over DeWitt Clinton.
       War with England ; attacks on Sackett's Harbor and
          Ogdensburg repulsed.
1813. Ogdensburg captured by the English : Sackett's Harbor
          successfully defended ; Buffalo burned.
       Gideon Hawley superintendent of common schools.
1814. Battle of Lake Champlain ; close of hostilities in New
          York.
1816. Money voted for beginning the Erie canal.
1817. DeWitt Clinton governor.
       Abolition of slavery after ten years decreed.
       The Erie canal begun.
1819. Canal navigation opened between Rome and Utica.
1821. Meeting of the constitutional convention.
1822. Adoption of the second constitution of New York.
1823. Joseph C. Yates governor.
       The Champlain canal completed.
1825. DeWitt Clinton again governor.
       Opening of the Erie canal.

PERIOD V.

CHAPTER XV.

PROSPERITY AND DISASTER.—1826–1846.

The twenty years following the completion of the Erie canal was a time of change. The last of the men of the Revolutionary period died. July fourth, 1826, the fiftieth anniversary of the Declaration of Independence, its writer, Thomas Jefferson, and its bold advocate, John Adams, both passed away; on independence day, four years later, Monroe died in the city of New York; and meanwhile New York's Revolutionary leader, John Jay, expired at a great age.

It was a time of rapidly growing towns, of the making of huge fortunes, of railroads begun and of telegraphs dreamed of. Before the onward rush of these twenty years the old families of New York city and the Hudson valley, whose power had partly survived the Revolution, passed completely into history; new blood flowed through the veins of the awakened State.

DeWitt Clinton was again made governor in the year after the opening of the Erie canal. He had new projects for the welfare of the State; he urged the legislature to improve the public schools, to establish schools to train teachers, to build more canals, to make a State highway through the southern counties. Toward the close of his term in the midst of his patriotic labors he suddenly died. After

(148)

a usual day's work at the capitol, while talking with his family, his head dropped forward and he was dead.

New York has given greater statesmen to the nation, but has produced no greater man for the State. His public life excepting a few months' service in the United States senate was given to New York. As mayor of New York city, as canal commissioner, and as governor he gained a national fame. He made the Erie canal; but he was not a man of one idea; he was the foremost champion of the common schools and of the proper treatment of criminals and insane. But this friend of mankind was cold and distant to men personally; with his imperious will he would brook no opposition; he made enemies in turn of such former friends as Robert R. Livingston, Daniel D. Tompkins and Martin Van Buren. But the sturdy honesty of his purpose is undoubted; and the State must honor him as it can honor no other.

The Elections of 1828.—After the death of DeWitt Clinton, Martin Van Buren was easily the leading man of the State; in the same year, 1828, he was elected governor. This was the year of a presidential election; and Van Buren bent all his energy to put General Jackson in the place of President Adams.

For the first time in the history of the State the presidential electors were chosen by the people. The electors, however, at this time were not all on a general State ticket as has since been the practice; but each congressional district chose one elector and the men thus elected appointed two more electors. In this way it happened that sixteen Adams electors were chosen and twenty Jackson electors.

The result in all the States was a large majority for the hero of New Orleans. President Jackson called Van Buren to be secretary of state; and thus the office of governor fell to Enos T. Throop, the lieutenant-governor. Governor Throop after filling Van Buren's term was, in 1830, elected by the people to the office, after a close contest with a new party known as the anti-masons.

The Anti-Masons.—William Morgan of Batavia, Genesee county, was a printer and belonged to the society of free-masons. In 1826 it became known in the town that he was about to publish a book telling the secrets of that order. Suddenly he disappeared ; great excitement and a search for the missing man followed. It was discovered that Morgan was arrested on a made-up charge and put in the Canandaigua jail. On his release he was seized by a party of masons and carried gagged and bound in a close carriage to Fort Niagara. At this point all trace of the man was lost ; but there is little doubt that he was put to death.

As this story came out exaggerated by wild rumors, there was great indignation at the murder of a free man. The excited citizens instead of bending all their efforts to punish the few men who did the deed, directed much of their feeling against the entire masonic order. Many of the masons in turn unwisely tried to make little of the great crime instead of seeking to bring the criminals to justice. A violent opposition to the masonic fraternity sprang up in western New York. The anti-masons, unable to find the murderers of Morgan or to convict those who carried him off, determined to punish all masons at the ballot-box ; and in town and county elections they succeeded in keeping masons from office. The excitement spread ; a convention was called, a party was organized for the purpose of driving the masonic order from the State ; and a State ticket was nominated which was barely defeated.

In 1830 the anti-masonic party polled one hundred and twenty thousand votes and lacked but eight thousand of electing their candidate for governor ; two years later the party was defeated in a similar manner, at a time when the feeling had so spread that a presidential candidate was nominated. But the infection died out of politics as suddenly as it arose.

Democrats and Whigs.—Little affected by the appearance of masonry in politics the national democratic party was solid and triumphant under the leadership of Martin Van Buren ; it gave the electors of New York to Jackson at his reëlection in 1832, and at the same time elected William L. Marcy governor of the State. Marcy was again chosen at the next two elections, and so was governor for six years.

At his second election the opponents of the democratic party first united under the name of whigs. Up to this time there had been no united opposition to the democrats in national affairs. The first whig candidate for governor of New York was William H. Seward of Auburn.

Two years later Martin Van Buren reached the height of his ambition by securing the presidency ; he was therefore the first man from New York to be elected president of the United States.

Prosperity and Hard Times.—Perhaps the success of Van Buren in political life was partly due to the prosperity of the times. There was rapid progress in the State and in the nation. On the banks of the Erie canal, where once was a wilderness, farms, villages and cities were appearing. Buffalo, all but two of whose two hundred houses had been burned by the English in 1813, was a city ; Rochester, which at the time of the same war was composed of one log house, had fifteen thousand people at the time of Van Buren's election to the presidency ; Utica was a newly made city and Syracuse was a promising village. Farmers received good prices ; mechanics were busy ; speculators doubled their money. So it was throughout the union ; people began to live beyond their means ; credit was easy ; but pay day came at last.

The panic of 1837 brought the first widespread hard times since the days of the embargo. New York city, the commercial centre, first felt the effect ; banks failed ; factories stopped ; overgrown

towns were half deserted.   Many States could not pay their debts;
New York had not credit enough to borrow a half million dollars
at six per cent.

The people blamed the party in power and the next year, 1838,

MARTIN VAN BUREN.

went over to the whigs in such
numbers as to elect William H.
Seward governor. President Van
Buren lost his hold on New York
and two years later when he was a
candidate for reëlection, he failed
to get the electors of his own State
and was defeated by William
Henry Harrison.   At the same
time Governor Seward was given
a second term.   It was at this
election of 1840 that mass meetings and parades were first used
by the political parties.

The Anti-Rent Rebellion.
—Meanwhile trouble within the
State claimed attention; eastern New York was disturbed.   From
the time of the Dutch patroon system much of the land in the
eastern counties was held by the families of the original owners,
who did not sell their farms but leased them at a small rent for a
long term of years.   In time the improvements made the farms
valuable, and the forgotten rents were demanded.   The farmers on
the leased lands were threatened with ruin; they banded together
to resist the collection of rents, drove off the sheriffs, and at Graf-
ton, Rensselaer county, killed one of the officers.   In the same year,
1839, fifteen hundred anti-renters gathered at Reidsville to resist
the sheriff and his men.   The counties of Albany, Rensselaer, Col-

umbia, Delaware, Greene and Schoharie were partly in a state of rebellion; western counties also, where the Holland land company owned large tracts, were stirred up to a less extent.

Governor Seward called out the militia, and secured quiet. Silas Wright, who succeeded to the office of governor after William C. Bouck's uneventful term, took hold of the anti-rent trouble with a firm hand. Many of the law-breakers were brought to trial and sent to prison.

Still there was some justice on the side of the anti-renters; they  had the sympathy of the people and uniting with the whigs in 1846 they defeated Silas Wright and elected John Young governor. Governor Young pardoned the fifty or more prisoners, and the State constitution adopted the same year forbade the leasing of land for long terms, and in other ways provided for the gradual cure of the evil.

The Patriot War.—The counties bordering on Canada also had their excitement during these years. Many of the Canadians were anxious for independence

SILAS WRIGHT.

from England and naturally received much sympathy from their neighbors across the St. Lawrence and Niagara rivers. Nearly a thousand zealous men of New York encamped on Navy island in the Niagara river, about two miles above the falls, using the steamboat "Caroline" to bring their provisions and arms. The English seized this vessel from its moorings on the American side and set it adrift over the falls.

The excitement and feeling against England among the people of the border counties were intense ; but Van Buren who was president at the time issued a proclamation of neutrality and sent General Scott to keep the peace.   Along the northern State line from Rouse's Point to Cape Vincent the sons of Revolutionary heroes were prepared at any time to cross into Canada to help the patriot cause ; they stole the arms from the arsenal at Watertown ; and for five or six years they made ineffectual raids across the river.

Highways and Railroads.—The southern tier of counties, though somewhat free from the excitement of the anti-mason, anti-rent and patriot war troubles, had their own topic of interest.   It was proposed to build a State road, a macadamised highway, from the Hudson river at Catskill, running through Ithaca and Bath to Buffalo.   DeWitt Clinton had urged this project not only to open up these counties, but as due them from the State in turn for taxes paid for the Erie canal,—an expense which had largely benefited the central counties.   The legislature defeated the bill year after year, until in 1836 to compromise matters it gave three million dollars of State money to help the building of the Erie railroad.

The first railroad in the State and one of the first passenger railroads in the United States was constructed of wooden rails from Albany to Schenectady, a distance of seventeen miles, in 1831. Ten years later the Erie railroad was opened from Piermont to Goshen.

Canals.—For a long time the growth of the railroads was not such as to lead people to think that they would take the place of canals ; and so the State continued to build water ways branching north and south from the Erie canal.   The Champlain canal, connecting the Hudson and Champlain valleys, was in operation three years before the completion of the Erie canal.   The Oswego canal and the Cayuga and Seneca canal were next constructed.   Then the State grew lavish and dug the Genesee valley, the Chemung and Black river canals, at great cost, only to abandon them in later years when railroads spread their net work over the State.

At first these canals carried passengers as well as freight ; passenger boats or packets, fitted with dining-rooms and sleeping berths and drawn by three or four horses, carried travelers at the rate of five miles an hour ; though so little dependence was to be put on these boats that it was a common saying that canal travel was at the rate of "a cent and a half a mile, a mile and a half an hour."

The carrying of freight was always the great business of the canals. Before the Erie canal was open it cost from fifty to one hundred dollars to transport a ton from Buffalo to Albany. The first boats cut this charge down to less than twenty dollars. In 1835 the rate fell to about five dollars ; and when in 1882 the State abolished the tolls and railroads were competing for the freight, grain was carried the length of the Erie canal for a dollar a ton.

New York City.—During the twenty years following 1825 the State increased over a million in population, and by 1850 had three million inhabitants. Of these, half a million were in New York city ; for great as had been the development of the interior, still more wonderful was the progress of the city. With magical rapidity the great blocks of brick and stone reached northward over Manhattan island. In 1845 the limit of continuous buildings reached Fourteenth street, where forty years later was the centre of the retail trade. In the lower part of the city, room was made by building upward ; blocks of three or four stories were replaced by those of six and eight floors ; and these in turn gave way to twelve and fourteen story buildings.

Generally throughout the city the old stood aside for the new. For lighting, whale oil began to give place to gas in 1825, much to the fear of timid ones who were afraid that the island would be blown up. Eight years later the horse cars first took the place of the lumbering stages. But the gas and horse cars were in turn to become old-fashioned in the dawning age of electricity. There was even then a certain artist in the city who was busy experimenting with electricity and coiling long strips of wire about his room. His name was Samuel F. B. Morse, and by 1844 he had made the magnetic telegraph a success.*

The news whether flashed by electricity or brought by slower means was nowhere put in more readable shape than in New York city. It was in the 'thirties and 'forties that the press of the metropolis took its place in the lead of the newspapers of America. William Cullen Bryant was editor of the Evening Post; Horace Greeley, after publishing the Log Cabin in the Harrison campaign of 1840, began the Tribune next year; James Gordon Bennett was filling the Herald with news; the brilliant Henry J. Raymond some years later started the Times; Thurlow Weed, whig and anti-mason, was publishing the Albany Evening Journal. The common price of a paper was six cents, when the Sun, the first of the one-cent papers, was started in 1833 and soon reached the unheard of circulation of six thousand a day. The magazine and book publishers began to gather at New York city and in time made it the literary centre of the continent.

The city was attracting keen men in every line of business. John Jacob Astor, in his day the richest man in America, was making money out of the Alaska fur trade; Peter Cooper was getting rich from the manufacture of glue; and Alexander T. Stewart was the first great merchant prince, imitated later by so many thousand of his countrymen. Wall street and Broadway became the goal of every ambitious young man in the country.

---

* In this connection it should be remembered that Cyrus W. Field, to whose energy and foresight the Atlantic cable is due, was a New Yorker. In 1854 he was working at the idea; in 1858 he had laid a cable; in 1866 he made the submarine telegraph a success.

The city also attracted the ignorant and brutal ; it took a part, often the worst part, of every ship-load of foreigners. As the rush of immigrants increased, the city was in constant danger from its ignorant mass of humanity. Riots were common ; mobs held the streets. Anti-slavery meetings were broken up by rioters ; during the panic, stores were entered for food and clothing ; and at the great Astor Place riot in 1856 it needed but the petty quarrel of some actors to stir the slums of the city to such bloody deeds that only volleys of musketry from the soldiers could scatter the mob. The police at these times were nearly powerless ; neither was it the perfection of the police system which changed the riotous New York city of before the war to the more orderly place of later years. Free public schools, Sunday schools, missions, asylums, hospitals, free baths and public parks have done what the law could not accomplish.

There were other checks to the progress of the city beside its riotous inhabitants. During one summer the cholera took possession of the city, threw the people into a panic and carried off three thousand victims. Soon after on a cold December night thirteen acres of buildings were burned. Both disasters were laid to the poor and insufficient supply of water, and hastened the building of the Croton aqueduct.

The lack of water had long been felt. The water from street wells and that distributed by a private company was unsatisfactory. Forty miles north in Westchester county is the Croton river. In 1835 the work of bringing this river into the homes and shops of New York city began. A lake was made by means of a great dam. From this reservoir the water was received by a granite aqueduct of circular shape about eight feet wide and seven feet high.

Through hills and over streams this huge pipe was built, until finally crossing the Harlem river by High bridge it reached the distributing reservoir covering one hundred and five acres in Central

park.   Seven years after the beginning of this work, on the fourth
of July, the water was let into the aqueduct, and the event duly celebrated.   The Croton aqueduct cost nine million dollars ; but vast
as was the scale on which it was built, within fifty years it could
not supply the multiplied population.*

A companion work of the Croton aqueduct in purifying New
York city was the Central park, which may be noticed here, though
it was begun several years later.   It was just before the civil war
that the city bought the land, two and a half miles long and half a
mile wide, out of which the famous park was made at an expense
of fifteen million dollars ; as much money as the United States paid
France for half the land west of the Mississippi.

A few years before Central park was begun, the city held a
world's fair in a great building called the Crystal palace.   This
immense house of glass contained a display which educated the
people and helped the trade and commerce of the city and country.
The shipping traffic of that port had so increased that two-thirds
of the foreign trade of the United States was carried on at New
York city.

The city as the gateway from the Atlantic was at various times
called upon to welcome distinguished men to the shores of America.
Its citizens did honor in 1825 to Lafayette on his visit to the scenes
of his early struggles ; later they welcomed Dickens and Thackeray
the novelists, Jenny Lind, the singer, Kossuth the Hungarian
patriot ; and most royally of all they feasted a citizen of their own
State, the greatest American man of letters, Washington Irving, on
his return from the court of Spain.

---

*The first Croton aqueduct supplied 95,000,000 gallons in twenty-four hours, or about
two hundred gallons for every man, woman and child in the city.   When the population
increased to over a million the water fell short.   An aqueduct to the Bronx river in 1884 in
creased the amount of water to 115,000,000 gallons daily.   The second Croton aqueduct was
begun in 1885 and finished in 1890.   It is built under ground, passing by a tunnel under the
Harlem river.   This aqueduct increases the supply to 315,000,000 gallons.   " Compared with
other tunnels, this new aqueduct is easily at the head of all works of a like character in the
world."   See the Century magazine for December, 1889, (Vol. 39).

CHAPTER XVI.

THE CONTEST FOR FREE SCHOOLS.—1847-1854.

At the close of the first half of the nineteenth century New York held the first place among the thirty-one States in population, agriculture, manufacture and commerce; but in education the State did not excel. The history of education in New York up to that time was in short this :—The Dutch did something for their schools; the English did less. At the close of the Revolution there was an awakening demand for better schools. In 1795 the first State appropriation for common schools was made; and ten years later a permanent fund was established. The school system, however, dates from 1813, when the office of superintendent of schools was created,—an office which after a few years became a department under the secretary of state.

DeWitt Clinton was a champion of the school system; he filled his messages to the legislature with pleas for normal schools, free schools, county superintendents and school libraries.

The Schools from 1825 to 1846.—In 1825 there were eight thousand common schools and nearly half a million pupils. Ten years afterward eight academies were chosen to instruct teachers' classes,—the first effort to provide properly qualified instructors. Another experiment, of which much was expected, was buying and distributing libraries to the school districts. Although many of the books thus sent out were scattered and lost, their good effect probably more than repaid the outlay.

Of the different secretaries of state, John A. Dix was especially active in advancing the interests of common schools, and his deputy,

(159)

Samuel S. Randall, was a faithful friend of education. In 1841 the office of county superintendent of schools was created. These superintendents were chosen by the county boards of supervisors; and this method of election gave a chance for political trickery. To remedy this defect the office was abolished after a short trial ; and for ten years longer there was no school officer between the deputy of the state superintendent and the district trustees. In 1856 the office of county superintendent was revived under the form of school commissioners elected by the people of the commissioner districts.

The pressing demand for trained teachers called forth the plan of holding teachers' institutes in the different counties of the State, and resulted in the establishing of a permanent school for teachers, the Albany Normal school.*

But the State remained without free schools. The separate districts could make their own schools free if they wished and some of the districts did so; but the State had no free school system compact and progressive. The common schools were in part supported by the fund growing out of the sale of public lands ; but the rest of the expense was paid by tuition in the shape of rate bills. These rate bills called upon those who sent children to pay according to the number of days they had been in attendance.

The Third State Constitution.—The advocates of free schools hoped to carry their point in the convention which met in 1846 to revise the constitution. The third constitution, which took the place of the second after it had been in effect for twenty-five years, made but little change in the executive State officers ; it provided that senators be elected by separate districts ; it remodeled the courts, formed the court of appeals and provided that many judges before appointed should be elected by the people ; it forbade long

---

*The name of the Albany Normal school, the first of the normal schools of the State, was changed in 1890 to the New York State Normal College.

leases of land, the banking monopoly,* and incurring of debts by the legislature.

A provision for free schools was included ; but on the last day of the session of the convention it was thrown out ; and so when the people voted to accept the proposed constitution they had no chance to show their opinion on the great question of free schools.

Free Schools Secured and Lost.—But the demand of the times was not to be denied ; the legislature of 1849 passed a bill making all the common schools of the State free. The law declared that each district should have suitable buildings, and conduct a school for at least four months of the year, open to all residents between the ages of five and twenty-one. Such a law was in the power of the legislature; but in order to test the opinion of the people it was submitted to a vote of the State and ratified by a tremendous majority.

The free-school act was put in force so awkwardly that the unusual taxes fell unequally upon the people of the State. Those who were satisfied kept still ; the dissatisfied made loud complaints. So after a year's trial but a small majority of the people stood by the law ; and the legislature at its next session weakened before the petitions of the growling taxpayers, repealed the bill, and brought back the system of rate bills.

Thus the lawmakers of the State continued to accept as good reasoning the argument of the childless taxpayer that he ought not to educate his neighbors' children, and failed to recognize the fact that educated voters alone make a good State, and that every man

---

* Up to the time of the panic of 1837 every bank had to have a charter from the legislature and the banking business became a monopoly in the hands of a favored few. In the time of Hamilton's power the federalists controlled all the banks of the State. Aaron Burr, under the guise of a bill to supply New York city with fresh water, secured a charter for the Manhattan bank, an institution still existing. The fortunes of DeWitt Clinton suffered from the connection of his friends with a paying bank monopoly. In 1800 there were two banks in New York city ; the number was increased to thirty in 1840, and reached one hundred in 1880.

who enjoys the benefits of the republic is in duty bound to pay for
the education of all its citizens. In these days the slavery question
was crowding out every other subject of importance ; and the State
was doomed to wait for its free schools until after the civil war. A
step in advance was taken in 1854, however, when the department
of education was set off by itself under a superintendent of public
instruction elected by the legislature for a term of three years, and
Victor M. Rice was made the first superintendent.

Governors.—Many of the successors of DeWitt Clinton in the
governor's chair were active school men. Governor Wright said in
a message : "No public fund of the State is so unpretending, yet
so all pervading ; so little seen yet so universally felt....as this
fund for the support of the common schools."

SCHOOL SUPERVISION IN NEW YORK.
(From an Address of Hon. Andrew S. Draper.)

Year	By State officer.	By county officers.	By city officers.	By town officers.
1795.				
1813.				
1841.				
1847.				
1851				
1856.				
1890.				

The governors of New York,
after Seward's administration of
four years, were changed each term
for eight successive elections.
William C. Bouck, Silas Wright,
John Young, Hamilton Fish,
Washington Hunt, Horatio Seymour, Myron H. Clark, and John
A. King filled the office from 1843
to 1859. Silas Wright* was one
of the ablest of these men; Horatio Seymour was for many years
prominent in public life; and Myron H. Clark is to be remembered
for receiving his election on a plat-
form favoring prohibition of the

---

* Silas Wright, a native of Massachusetts, filled many important offices in New York,
and acquired a national reputation in the United States senate. He refused a nomination
as candidate for the vice-presidency and a position in Polk's cabinet, and died in retirement
at Canton, 1847. See portrait, page 153.

liquor traffic.   The sale of liquor was in 1855 accordingly forbidden; but the law was not enforced and was soon repealed.

Many of these governors also served in the United States senate. Marcy, Wright, Seward and Fish were in the national senate before the war, and Daniel S. Dickinson, not a governor, was a distinguished senator at that time.

The Progress of the People of the State is suggested by the close of the first half of the nineteenth century. The western counties, which in 1800 were the great west of the immigrants from New England, later sent their own citizens to fill the caravans crossing the Mississippi. The stream from New York swelled to a torrent in 1849 when gold was discovered in California. But the population of New York continued to increase; the one million of 1800 had become four million in 1850. Chemung, Fulton and Wyoming counties were organized after 1825 and "little Schuyler," in 1854 made the number of counties an even sixty.

The progress of invention has been so great that the people of the latter half of the century know almost as little of the daily life of those who lived in the 'twenties and 'thirties as of those who lived in the Revolution. The sons do not realize that in the boyhood of their fathers matches were not known, that thirty or forty miles was a day's journey, that it cost eighteen cents to send a letter from one end of the State to the other, that often the result of an election was not known until a month after the voting, that watches were hardly known except among the rich, that the school houses and the school books were of the rudest kinds.

There were indications of an improvement in the morals of the people. Lotteries were forbidden; imprisonment for debt was abolished; suitable State prisons at Sing Sing and Auburn were provided; prisoners were not only punished but taught how to work; asylums for the insane, blind, dumb and helpless increased, some built by State aid, some by religious societies. The Christian church was an increasing power. Many revivals of religion awakened deep feeling throughout the State during the fifty years of the century. Many of the successors of Everardus Bogardus the first minister of New York, have been famous preachers, among them Henry Ward Beecher, of Brooklyn, and E. H. Chapin of New York city.

Peculiar People.—The State seemed to have more than its share of people with strange religious and social beliefs. At Watervliet (wa-ter-vleet), near Albany, the first communities of "Shakers" in the United States under Mother Ann Lee settled, and from thence they sent colonies to Columbia and Livingston counties. At Palmyra, Wayne county, Joseph Smith lived, who pretended to find buried there the book of Mormon ; and from that place his followers began their westward march, which ended at Salt Lake city.

In Yates county, on the shores of Seneca and Keuka lakes, Jemima Wilkinson, the " Universal Friend," lived in the first frame house in western New York, and gathered her followers about her. In Low Hampton, Washington county, lived the farmer-preacher, William Miller, who taught the speedy coming of the end of the world, and in 1843 he and fifty thousand converts waited expectantly for the second coming of Christ. In Madison county, John H. Noyes established in 1847 the Oneida community, for a time peculiar in some of its practices, but now a mere business association.

At North Elba, in Essex county, lived John Brown before the border warfare in Kansas and the raid on Harper's Ferry ; and there in the soil of New York his body lies mouldering in the grave while his soul goes marching on.

CHAPTER XVII.

NEW YORK DURING THE STRUGGLE WITH SLAVERY.—1855–1869.

From 1821 to 1854.—About the time that slavery was abolished in New York, it became the leading political topic in national politics. New York protested against the admission of Missouri as a slave State in 1821; but while the people of New York generally expressed themselves against the admission of more slave territory, those who advocated the removal of slavery from the country were few and despised. In 1835 six hundred delegates to an anti-slavery convention at Utica were driven out of town.

The increasing friction between the free and slave States was shown five years later, when the governor of Virginia demanded of William H. Seward, governor of New York, three men charged with stealing a negro from slavery. Governor Seward refused on the ground that slave stealing was not a crime in New York. Some years later eight slaves owned in Virginia were set at liberty in New York city and escaped to Canada.

The sentiment of the people of New York was against the admission of Texas and against the resulting Mexican war waged in 1846 and 1847 in the interest of the extension of slavery territory. The State also opposed the compromise of 1850 when the fugitive slave law was passed, compelling free States to arrest and return escaped negroes. This law brought on the contest; States could not be joined under one flag, while slavery was allowed by some commonwealths and was a crime in others.

Slavery in Politics.—By this time questions of State interest, which since 1815 had taken the attention of political parties, gave

(165)

way to the great national slavery agitation. The whig party, not daring to take sides, died out; the republican party, opposed to the extension of slavery, was born. The first presidential candidate of that party, John C. Fremont, received the electoral votes of New York, but was defeated by the democratic nominee, James Buchanan.

At the same election John A. King, a republican, was chosen governor; he after one term gave way to Edwin D. Morgan of the same party, who afterward earned the title of the war governor of New York. The different State elections in the year of Morgan's first election, 1858, foretold the triumph of the new party in the coming national election of 1860.

In the exciting canvass of that year William H. Seward was the

most prominent man of his party and was supported by the delegates from his State at the republican national convention. Seward, however, was set aside, largely through the efforts of Horace Greeley, editor of the New York Tribune, and Abraham Lincoln of Illinois was nominated for president. The admirers of the great anti-slavery statesman of New York were keenly disappointed; but they heartily helped to elect Lincoln and viewed with pride the illustrious services of William H. Seward as secretary of state during the perilous civil war.

WILLIAM H. SEWARD.

New York Responds to the Call.—The election of Abraham Lincoln was the signal for the long threatened rebellion of the

south ; South Carolina led off.   The New York legislature promptly offered the national government money and men to aid in forcing
South Carolina to remain in the union.   But this was in the first
weeks of 1861 ; Buchanan was still president and made no effort
to put down the rising rebellion.

In New York city and throughout the State there were long
petitions and large mass meetings calling for peace at any price ;
and there were other petitions and mass meetings demanding the
preservation of the union at all hazards.   It was plain that New
York city, through which passed two-thirds of the revenue of the
United States, would suffer most from war ; to the citizens of that
city peace meant plenty, war threatened bankruptcy.

The ignorant masses of the poorer streets could be relied upon to
favor slavery ; the mayor himself had the effrontery to propose that
the metropolis secede from the State and nation and become a
free city.   Thus the southern States came to look to New York for
help as the English had done a hundred years before.

In this the slave power was disappointed.   When Sumter fell the
loyal city and State awoke.   When Lincoln shortly after his inauguration called for seventy-five thousand soldiers, New York, whose
share was thirteen thousand, sent thirty thousand troops.   On the
nineteenth of April, the anniversary of the battle of Lexington,
the famous seventh regiment marched down Broadway to the cheers
of loyal thousands.

Soon in that eventful first year of civil strife the news of the
defeat at Bull Run came ; then the State seemed of one mind :
thousands poured into the recruiting stations at New York city and
Elmira ; old men and boys concealed their ages that they might
enlist ; town and State authorities added to the pay given by the
government ; the mothers and sisters gathered in bands and societies to make the comforts of home for the field and hospital ; the

State loaned and gave money to the national government by the
million; the stars and stripes suddenly blossomed out from house-
top, window and pole. By the end of the year 1861 New York had
sent one hundred and twenty thousand men into the field, one out
of every six of the able-bodied men of the State. At the close of
the campaign of 1862 there were two hundred and fifty thousand
of her men on the field scattered over nine different States of the
south.

Reverses.—But a reaction set in. In the great plenty of supplies there were waste, stealing and mismanagement. The democratic party criticised the way in which the war was carried on,
and in the fall of 1862 they elected as governor, Horatio Seymour,
who ten years before had held the same office. Governor Seymour,
while he believed that the war could be ended, was loyal to the
preservation of the union.

The result of the second year of the war was not reassuring to the
north. Some progress was made in the Mississippi valley; but
McClellan in the peninsular campaign failed to take Richmond and
exposed Washington to danger.

The gloom deepened as 1863 began. The defeats of the northern
army at Fredericksburg and Chancellorsville left the north open to
the victorious army of Lee. The anti-war party of New York grew
strong; recruits were no longer plentiful; and when a draft was
ordered, angry mutterings filled the air. New York city was the
centre of the disturbance. There on the fourth of July the opponents of the war held a mass meeting. They denounced the president and the generals; they declared the war a failure. On that
day Vicksburg surrendered, the Mississippi was opened to the gun-
boats of the north, and Lee was hurrying south from his defeat at
Gettysburg.

The Draft Riot of 1863.—A few days later the draft began in
New York city, and all the pent-up wrath of the southern sympa-

thizers broke forth. The mob swept over the city like fire, burning, plundering and murdering. The negroes were the especial victims ; many of them were killed ; an orphan asylum for negroes was burned. For three days the rioters held the city ; traffic stopped ; stores were closed ; houses were barricaded ; the police were powerless, and no soldiers were at hand.

When at length order was restored, one thousand persons had been killed and wounded and two million dollars worth of property destroyed. The draft was then resumed under the protection of troops. The next year a band of men was discovered preparing to set fire to the principal hotels and public buildings of the city ; this was probably part of a plot to burn and plunder the large cities of the north.

The End and the Result.—The victories of 1864 promised peace ; but a battle at the ballot-boxes remained to be fought in New York and in other loyal States. The republican party was victorious ; Lincoln received the votes of nearly all the northern States ; and Reuben E. Fenton was elected governor of New York.

When the war closed in the spring of 1865, New York had furnished to the union within a few thousand of one half-million soldiers, or about one-fifth of the number of men who entered the federal army. By the end of that year nearly all the surviving soldiers were again at work on their farms, in the shops and the stores.

But the terrible loss of war was everywhere felt. The death of Lincoln, the broken families, the bitter feeling arising from party strife were all a part of the price paid for the union. The census of 1865 showed, for the first time in any five years in the history of the State, a decrease in the population, amounting to fifty thousand people.

The fifteenth amendment to the constitution of the United States gave to the negro the right to vote, and thus embodied the result of the war ; it was ratified by the legislature of New York in 1869. The State had never removed the property qualification of two hundred and fifty dollars imposed upon the negroes in 1822. At different times before the war the people voted down the proposition to repeal this law, and even after the war they again decided against the repeal, so that the negro in New York gained his equal rights by the constitution of the general government and not by the act of the citizens of the State.

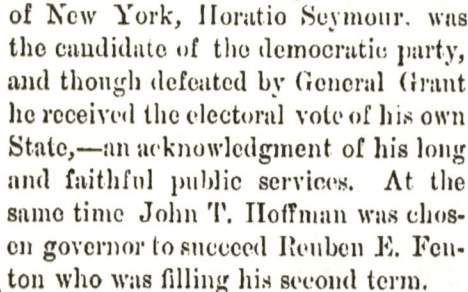

In the presidential election of 1868 another distinguished citizen of New York, Horatio Seymour, was the candidate of the democratic party, and though defeated by General Grant he received the electoral vote of his own State,—an acknowledgment of his long and faithful public services. At the same time John T. Hoffman was chosen governor to succeed Reuben E. Fenton who was filling his second term.

HORATIO SEYMOUR.

Education.—The year 1867 marks the throwing open of all the common schools of the State ; thus did New York tardily make its public schools free. The Albany normal school, and the Oswego normal school, which was begun in war times, were made free, and six other normal schools were soon after organized.

Cornell university was founded at the same time largely by State aid. This school, though one of the youngest colleges of the State, was destined soon to outstrip the older schools in number of students and in wealth.

The regents of the university adopted a plan of examinations to be held in the higher schools of the State, and have since distributed the money in their charge according to the number of pupils in each institution who have passed them successfully. The result has been an increase in the number of schools between the district schools and colleges until nearly every village of the State has its academy or academic department of a union school.

CHAPTER XVIII.

THE ERA OF CENTENNIALS.—1870-1889.

The twenty-five years following the civil war include the end of the first one hundred years of the life of the State. The true history of this period cannot be told in the nineteenth century.

Parties and Elections.—In political matters the State has been a pendulum, now swinging to the democratic and now to the republican side. The majority at each vote for president has alternated from one party to the other since 1864. The legislatures have for the most part been republican; the governor during sixteen years of the time has been a democrat.

Governor Hoffman was reëlected in 1870; but two years later the republicans made John A. Dix governor. General Dix held important State offices before the war and as secretary of the treasury under Buchanan sent to New Orleans the famous dispatch,—"If any man dares to haul down the American flag, shoot him on the spot." Large as was his majority for governor, the vote was as decidedly the other way two years later, when he was defeated by Samuel J. Tilden.

In the centennial year when Tilden was a candidate for president, Lucius Robinson, also of the democratic party, was elected governor. At this time the term of office was again made three years. At the end of Robinson's administration a division in the democratic party gave the office to Alonzo B. Cornell, the republican candidate. But when the next election came, in 1882, a greater division in the republican party gave Grover Cleveland a majority of nearly two hundred thousand, the largest ever given a governor of the State. This office proved to Cleveland the stepping-stone to the presidency, and David B. Hill, the lieutenant-governor, served the last year of Cleveland's term and twice after was elected to the same position.

At every presidential election during the quarter-century following the was at least one of the candidates of the two leading parties for president or vice-president has been from New York ; at five of the six elections the candidate of the democratic party for president has been from New York ; and the three republican vice-presidents elected since Grant's administration were from this State.

In 1872 Horace Greeley was defeated by General Grant, and died a few days later. At the election of 1876 Tilden, fresh from his triumphs over the Tweed ring and the canal ring, was declared by an electoral commission to be defeated.

William A. Wheeler, of New York, was vice-president under Hayes; he was succeeded as presiding officer of the senate by Chester A. Arthur, of the same State. In the senate the two most notable representatives of New York after the war were Roscoe Conkling and William M. Evarts. By the assassination of Garfield, Arthur became president ; and he was succeeded on the fourth of March, 1885, by Grover Cleveland, the fourth president and second elected to that office from New York.

During these twenty-five years the greenback party and various labor parties drew off many voters from the democrats and republicans for short periods. The prohibition party also controlled a small but increasing band of voters and kept the temperance question prominent in politics.

The Tweed Ring.—The State after the war became more than ever the centre of the political strife of the nation. Fraud, corruption and waste of the people's money were attending evils. In 1871 the country was astounded by the exposure of the Tweed frauds.

William II. Tweed secured control of the government of New York city. With the help of the mayor of the city and other shrewd officials he obtained large sums for work n... 'r done and in a short time plundered the city of about twenty million dollars.

By chance the evidence of his guilt was thrown in the way of the New York Times. Exposure followed. But the Tweed ring held all the offices, controlled the courts and defied conviction. The press of the city stirred up the people; the wrath of a deceived people crushed the ring.

Tweed was arrested; he escaped from jail and was afterward caught in Spain. He died in prison in April, 1878, within ten years after he had dictated the laws and elections of the city and State.

Following the disclosure of the Tweed frauds came the panic of 1873, the third time of financial distress and ruin within the century. As before, the business of New York city first felt the shock.

New York City.—The growth of the metropolis was hardly checked; the population was one and a quarter million in 1880 and still continued to increase rapidly toward the second million.

The stages and horse cars became utterly unable to carry the people back and forth, and the elevated railroads were opened in 1878 after much opposition. These fast trains gave new life to the upper part of the city, and yet within a dozen years they could not comfortably carry the increasing throngs and satisfy the demand for rapid transit. The stream of business men crossing East river to lower Manhattan island also had to be provided for, and the Brooklyn bridge, the largest suspension bridge in the world, was begun in 1870 and finished thirteen years later.

Scarcely less imposing than this bridge to the traveler entering the bay is the statue of Liberty, the gift of France, which, torch in hand, was set in 1886 to light the harbor of New York.

Wonders of Art and of Nature.—Up the river at Poughkeep-sie another great bridge was stretched across the Hudson, over which the coal of Pennsylvania goes to feed the fires of New England. At Albany the corner-stone of one of the most costly buildings in the world, the State capitol, was laid in 1871. The immense pile consumed twenty million dollars and still unfinished was occupied by the offices of the State government. Its wasteful elegance tells the story of many disgraceful deeds.

New York did a notable act when it freed its great natural wonder, the Niagara Falls, from the money-getters surrounding it, and made a public park of the land on the eastern side. In a like spirit of improvement the legislature went tardily to work to make a State park in the Adirondacks, to preserve the forests and to control the sources of the Hudson.

As the State grew older the beauty of its scenery was appreciated and increasing streams of sight-seers viewed the Palisades, the falls of the Genesee at Portage, the West Canada creek at Trenton falls, the Thousand Islands, the many inland lakes, the Catskills, the Adirondacks, the Watkins Glen.

The summer resorts of the State have become famous; the sea beaches of Long Island are filled; the summer schools and meetings at Chautauqua are thronged; mineral waters are sought at Clifton and at Richfield; and about the springs to which the Indians carried Sir William Johnson, the village of Saratoga Springs with its thirteen thousand people has sprung up.

Lessons from the Census.—The census of 1880, taken at the beginning of the second century of the State, supplies figures to estimate its progress among the commonwealths of the union. For sixty years the State had held the first place in population and had then five million inhabitants. While New York in extent of territory was not quite one-sixtieth of the United States, it had one-tenth of the population, one-half of whom lived in the twenty-five cities.* There were then but about twelve nations of the world with a population greater than that of New York.

More than two-thirds of the foreign traffic of the nation enters the harbor of the State, while in shipping and ship-owning New York represents from one-fourth to one-third of the total values of the United States. Its harbors, its bordering lakes, its large rivers, and its canals costing up to 1880 a round hundred million dollars, give to the State the rank which the same territory had among the Indians, and promise the primacy of New York among the States during the twentieth century.

Another well developed resource of the State is its fertile soil. In 1880 one-half of the land was under cultivation. The products were as varied as they were vast. In grain it ranked among the first States ; it raised one-seventh of the hay and one-fifth of the potatoes of the United States. Its hop area, centering in Madison and Oneida counties, produced four-fifths of the nation's crop. The vine-covered banks of the Hudson and of the central lakes yielded a considerable grape crop ; while its orchards and gardens from the flats of the Genesee to the Hudson valley produced no less abundance of other fruits.

In butter and cheese making the State was far in advance of any other ; in fact so diversified has become the product of the soil that the failure of one crop can have but little effect upon the productions of the entire State.

Another source of wealth is manufacturing ; in this New York again leads the union ; it had invested in 1880 from one-sixth to one-fifth of all the money employed in manufacturing in the United States. The manufactures are as varied as the crops. In agricultural implements, in ready-made clothing, in foundry products, furniture, pianos, jewelry, books, soap, refined sugar, and in

---

* The number of cities in 1890 was thirty-two.

a long list of other articles the State makes from one-sixth to more than a half of the entire national product.

These industries are not confined to New York city, but are spread over the State ; in Onondaga county salt is produced by the government ; in Fulton county gloves and mittens are made ; in Rensselaer, shirts and furnishing goods for men ; paper in Saratoga and Jefferson counties ; farming implements in Cayuga ; beer in Kings : cotton and woolen goods in Albany and Oneida : leather in Cattaraugus ; butter and cheese in many counties, led by Oneida, Herkimer, St. Lawrence, Delaware and Cattaraugus.

Schools.—New York has done much in later years to make its system of education a model ; though it was slow to feel the need of free schools, progress since the free school act has been rapid. The three colleges of the first years of the century had increased to twenty-seven in 1880, three of which were exclusively for women. The eight academies of 1800 had become nearly three hundred in number under the care of the regents of the university, including high schools and academic departments of union schools.

But the hope and glory of the State must rest in its common schools ; beyond these the mass of the people never go. In 1880 there were eleven thousand school districts ; and ten years later the expenditure for common schools was nearly twenty million dollars. The normal schools for the training of teachers were increasing and in 1890 had reached the number of eleven.

The money given in these years to educational purposes may have been sometimes unwisely distributed ; but compared with other public outlays the school money has been well expended and has produced good results. A uniform system of examining and licensing teachers has been secured by Superintendent Andrew S. Draper, and has proved helpful to the cause of good schools ; an unenforced compulsory education law has been passed,—a promise of a more efficient act to come.

At the End of a Century.—The people of New York have also advanced in a knowledge of the history of their State; books and magazines devoted to this branch of history have appeared, and there has been a growing appreciation of the great part which the colony and State played in the progress of America.

A patriotic love for the scenes of Revolutionary events and the memory of the early heroes have been fostered by centennial celebrations. The State was represented at the world's fair at Philadelphia in 1876, which commemorated the close of the first hundred years of independence. Other celebrations marked the centennial anniversaries of the struggle at Oriskany, at Saratoga, at Elmira and at Cherry Valley.

And finally at New York city, where Washington became president, the greatest celebration of all, April 30, 1889, did honor to the centenary of the birth of the constitution,—that strong bond of union, to make which New York gave up more than any other State, and from which it gained that advancement which makes it indeed the EMPIRE STATE.

SUMMARY OF EVENTS,—PERIOD V.

1826. Abduction of Morgan.

1828. Death of DeWitt Clinton.

1829. Martin Van Buren governor.
       Enos T. Throop governor.

1831. First railroad in the State from Albany to Schenectady.

1832. Great cholera year in New York city.

1833. William L. Marcy governor.

1836. Martin Van Buren elected president.

1837. Financial panic.
       Outbreak of the Patriot war.

1839. William H. Seward governor.
       Anti-rent trouble.

1841. Erie railroad open to Goshen.
1842. Croton aqueduct completed.
1843. William C. Bouck governor.
1845. Silas Wright governor.

1846. Third State constitution adopted.
1847. John Young governor.
1849. Hamilton Fish governor.
        Free school law passed ; (repealed, 1851).
1851. Washington Hunt governor.
1853. Horatio Seymour governor.
1855. Myron H. Clark governor.
        Prohibition law passed.
1857. John A. King governor.
1859. Edwin D. Morgan governor.
1861. Beginning of the civil war ; 120,000 troops sent by New
        York.
1862. The enlarged Erie canal completed.
1863. Horatio Seymour again governor.
        Draft riots in New York city.
1865. Reuben E. Fenton governor.
        End of the civil war.
1867. The common schools of the State made free.
1869. John T. Hoffman governor.
        Fifteenth amendment to the constitution of the United
        States ratified by New York.
1871. The corner stone of the capitol at Albany laid.
        Exposure of the Tweed frauds.
1873. John A. Dix governor.

1875. Samuel J. Tilden governor.

1877. Lucius Robinson governor.

1880. Alonzo B. Cornell governor.

1883. Grover Cleveland governor.
      Brooklyn bridge completed.

1883. Grover Cleveland elected president.

1885. David B. Hill governor.
      A State park made at Niagara Falls.

1886. Statue of liberty erected on Bedloe island.

1888. Great snow storm in New York city.

1889. Centennial celebration of Washington's inauguration.

1892. Roswell P. Flower governor.

1894. Adoption of Amendments to Constitution.

1895. Levi P. Morton governor.

APPENDIX.

QUESTIONS.

(The following questions on the text of this volume have been prepared for those teachers and pupils who may wish to make use of them.)

CHAPTER I.

1. Who is called the discoverer of New York?
2. Has any one else a claim to this title?
3. Name the five tribes of the Iroquois.
4. In what ways were they superior to other Indians?
5. Why had they chosen New York for their home?
6. What Indian tribes occupied the northern and eastern parts?
7. Of what foreign power did they implore aid and for what purpose?
8. Describe Champlain's expedition in 1609.
9. What was the result of his victory?
10. Name and give the extent of the five periods in the history of New York State.

PERIOD I.

CHAPTER II.

1. Give the date of Hudson's discovery of New York bay.
2. Of what nationality was he and in whose service?
3. To what country was he bound? What did he think the Hudson river might be?
4. About how far up the river did he sail?
5. Describe his death.

(181)

6. What two European nations besides the Spanish had colonies in America?

7. Where were these and in what condition?

8. What year is given as the date of the settlement of New York?

9. What was the object of the Dutch who first came to New York?

10. Why were Cape May and Block Island so called?

11. What are the modern names of the South, the Fresh, and the North rivers?

12. What name did the Dutch give their possessions in America?

13. How much land did they claim and how did they afterward modify this claim?

14. Who were the first Europeans to make New Netherland their home and where did they settle?

15. What company controlled New Netherland and what powers did it have?

16. Describe the patroon system of settlement.

17. Who was the first governor and when did he begin to rule?

18. Who appointed the other officers of the colony?

19. Name the three other governors under Dutch rule and give some characteristics of their rule.

20. Describe the manner in which the Dutch treated the Indians.

21. How did the first serious trouble with them arise?

22. Describe the Indian war.

23. What parts of the State were settled at the time of Minuet's administration?

24. From what countries of Europe did the settlers come?

25. Why did the people come from New England to New Netherland?

26. When were slaves first brought in?

27. Who was the last of the Dutch governors and how did he compare with the others?

28. Name the four difficulties confronting him? Which was the most serious?

29. Describe the Swede settlement on Delaware Bay.

30. How did Stuyvesant's treatment of the Indians differ from Kieft's?

31. What had the English done in Connecticut before Stuyvesant arrived?

32. What agreement did they make with him?

33. Give an illustration of the contempt of the English for the Dutch.

34. How did the condition of the people of Netherland compare with that of the people of New England?

35. What effect did the knowledge of this difference have on the Dutch settlers?

36. What was the first representative body of the people of the State called and under whose rule did it first meet? How much real power did it have?
37. Describe the surrender to the English.
38. Where did Stuyvesant afterwards live and die?

CHAPTER III.

1. What position did Holland hold among the European powers at this time?
2. What were the claims of the Dutch to New York? Of the English?
3. Why did the Dutch lose New York?
4. Tell what you can of David Pietersen de Vries and Arendt Van Curler.
5. What minister was prominent as a champion of the people?
6. Give the general characteristics of the common people.
7. Describe some of the punishments used.
8. Describe the Dutch houses.
9. Tell something of the life of the people.
10. Describe the dress of the men and women.
11. What was the government religion?
12. Name other denominations found in the colony.
13. Who was the first minister?
14. Tell something of the pay and position of the ministers.
15. Tell about the first schoolmaster and his duties.
16. What provision was made for education?
17. Name some modern customs which were derived from the Dutch.
18. What else have we obtained from them?

PERIOD II.

CHAPTER IV.

1. Where did the Puritans at first wish to land?
2. What title had the Duke of York to New Netherland?
3. What means did he take to secure it?
4. Did the English drive out the Dutch?
5. What changes were made in the names of places and of officers?

6. Did the colonists have the same rights under English rule that the New England colonies possessed?

7. Who was the first English governor?

8. How did his power compare with that of the Dutch governors?

9. What characteristic did he have which they lacked?

10. What difficulties did he meet?

11. How was the boundary between Connecticut and New York settled?

12. What was done with what are now the States of New Jersey and Delaware?

13. What became of Nichols?

14. Who took his place, and how was he regarded?

15. How were the Indians treated by the first English governors?

16. Tell something of the condition of the colony under Lovelace.

17. What led the Dutch to make an attack on New York city?

18. Did the Dutch residents help defend the city?

19. In what ways had the rule of the English disappointed them?

20. Who was in command of the Dutch fleet? Of the city?

21. Describe the attack.

22. Why was the capture by the Dutch fairer than that by the English nine years before?

23. Who was put in command of the colony?

24. Why did the Dutch give New York back to the English?

25. Who was the next governor, and how did he show his activity?

26. What was the population of the colony at this time? Of New York city?

27. What act had built up this city at the expense of the others?

28. Give a description of the city.

29. Tell something of Long Island and Brooklyn.

30. How did their education compare with what it had been under Dutch rule?

31. Tell something of their punishments.

32. What was generally used for money?

33. What were the chief exports?

34. What were the duties on imports?

35. Why was Andros recalled and who succeeded him?

36. How did Dongan compare with former governors?

37. What was his first act?

38. What was the date of the first charter of New York, and what were its chief provisions?

39. What did the Duke require of the assembly in return for this charter?
40. How did he keep his pledge with them?
41. What union of colonies was formed?
42. Who was sent as governor of the colonies, and who as lieutenant-governor of New York?
43. What two parties were growing up in the colony?
44. What change took place in England at this time, and how did this affect the colonists?
45. Who assumed the duties of governor and how did he come to do so?
46. Tell something of his administration.
47. What governor was appointed by the new king?
48. What led to the arrest of Leisler, and how was his death warrant obtained?
49. Give an account of his death.
50. How was he afterwards regarded?

CHAPTER V.

1. What was the disputed territory between New France and New York?
2. What claim had each to this?
3. Give an account of Isaac Jogues and La Moyne.
4. Tell something of the condition of the Iroquois.
5. What progress did the Jesuits make?
6. Describe the French invasion of New York.
7. Why did the French covet the Hudson Valley?
8. What expedition did they make into Western New York?
9. What fort did they build and with what result?
10. Tell what you can of Count Frontenac.
11. Give an account of the burning of Schenectady.
12. Mention other raids of the French in the following years.
13. Who was the most notable leader of New York forces, and what did he do?
14. What was done in Queen Anne's War?
15. What were the strong and the weak points of the French and English as shown in these wars?

CHAPTER VI.

1. What names were given to the two political parties in New York, and why?

2. Tell something of Fletcher.

3. Give an account of the trouble with the pirates.   Who was Captain Kidd?

4. Who followed Fletcher, and which party did he favor?

5. How was the assembly chosen at this time and of how many did it consist?

6. Who came as governor after Bellomont's death and how did he compare with Bellomont?

7. How did the dispute between the people and the government of England arise?

8. What power did the assembly hold over the governors?

9. Tell about the salary of the governors.

10. Name the four leading men of the colony.

11. Illustrate the way in which Cornbury made himself disliked.

12. Who is the next governor mentioned?

13. Give the population of the colony during the eighteenth century.

14. What parts were settled?

15. Give an account of the the colonization scheme of Governor Hunter.

16. What advantage did the English have over the French in the trade with the Indians?

17. What governor followed Hunter and what can you say of him?

18. What steps did he take to defeat the attempts of the French?

19. How was he hindered and in what ways did he become unpopular?

20. Give some account of Governor Cosby.

21. Tell about the first printing press and the newspaper published in the colony.

22. What was the cause of starting an opposition paper?

23. On what charge was Zenger arrested?

24. Give an account of his trial.

25. Name an important result of the verdict of this trial.

26. Who became acting governor after Cosby's death?

27. What did the assembly say to him?

28. How did he and other governors become wealthy?

29. About how many negroes were there in New York city?

30. What charge had been made against the negroes years before?

31. Give an account of the Negro Plot of 1741.

32. Were any white persons implicated?

33. Who succeeded Clarke?

34. What did the assembly refuse him and what did they demand?

CHAPTER VII.

1. Give some account of King George's war.
2. Why were not the advance posts of New York better protected?
3. How did the French break the treaty made after this war?
4. Why was the Albany convention called?
5. What colonies were represented?
6. What proposal was made by Benjamin Franklin?
7. In what year did the French and Indian war begin?
8. Tell what you can of the cause of this war?
9. Give an account of Shirley's Expedition.
10. Name the two forts held by each side in north-eastern New York.
11. What was the one victory of the English in 1755?
12. What new leader was sent to the French the next year and what did he do?
13. How did this affect the Iroquois?
14. How were the soldiers of the colony regarded by the English troops?
15. Describe the surrender of Fort William Henry.
16. How was the following winter spent?
17. Give an account of Abercrombie's attack on Fort Ticonderoga.
18. How was Fort Frontenac taken and with what result?
19. What general was sent out by the English and what fortress did he capture?
20. How was the war finished?
21. What was the result of the war?
22. In what ways had it helped the colonists?
23. Name some of the cities which grew up around forts.

CHAPTER VIII.

1. Name the counties of Long Island.
2. How did the settlers of the eastern part of the island differ from those in the rest of the colony?
3. What can you say of the settlement of the western part of Long Island?
4. Describe New York city.
5. What was its population?
6. How did it compare in importance with the rest of the State?
7. What had been the established church during Dutch rule?
8. What was the favored church under English rule?
9. Name some other denominations found in the colony

10. Tell about the public buildings of the city.

11. What and where was the first college of the State?

12. What was the condition of education under English rule?

13. Tell something of the southern Hudson counties.

14. Describe the counties along the Hudson.

15. Give some idea of the extent of Albany county, and name some of the villages.

16. Tell something of the ways of traveling, of the mails, the life of the common people and the manner of dress.

17. Name some of the great families of the State and tell how they lived.

18. How many acting governors did New York have in the century before the Revolution?

19. Give some reasons for the frequent changes.

20. Tell what you can of Sir William Johnson.

CHAPTER IX.

1. What were the navigation laws and their effect upon the colonies?

2. What is meant by the Stamp Act, and when was it passed?

3. What effect had this on the colonists?

4. Why was it so strongly opposed?

5. How were the colonies united?

6. What did the colonial congress of 1765 do?

7. Give an account of November 1, 1765.

8. Was the Stamp Act ever enforced?

9. What was the Quartering Act?

10. Give an account of the liberty poles of New York city.

11. What were non-importation societies, and why were they formed?

12. What bill did parliament wish the assembly to pass?

13. How did the English try to force the assembly to do this, and with what result?

14. What were the names given to the two parties in the colony?

15. Give some account of the troubles with the Indians.

16. Why would a general uprising of the Indians of the State have been especially dangerous at this time?

17. How was the boundary between Connecticut and New York decided?

18. What led to the contest between New Hampshire and New York?

19. By whom was it settled and in whose favor?

20. What reaction was there, and what kind of an assembly was chosen?

21. How did the new assembly displease the people?

22. How did the soldiers irritate the people, and what celebrated fight occurred?

23. Under what circumstances was trade with England resumed?

24. Why had New York suffered more than the other colonies from non-importation?

25. For what is Lord Dunmore's administration noticeable?

26. Who was the last English governor?

27. What was England's last attempt to enforce taxation?

28. What was the plan of parliament after the failure with the tea tax?

29. What port was closed?

30. Tell of the three parties in New York. Which was the strongest?

31. Did the New York assembly endorse the action of the first Continental Congress?

32. Tell something of the feeling of the people.

33. What was the effect of the news of the battle of Lexington?

PERIOD III.

CHAPTER X.

1. Give an account of the capture of Fort Ticonderoga.

2. How did the Green mountain boys happen to be organized?

3. What congress met on the same day?

4. Which side did most of the Indians support?

5. How many men was New York called to furnish at first?

6. What two men of the State were appointed generals?

7. Tell what you can of Montgomery.

8. After the English were driven from Boston, where were they expected?

9. Did Washington hope to keep them out of the city?

10. What steps were taken toward a State government at this time?

11. How was the Declaration of Independence received?

12. What battle was fought before the English took possession of New York city?

13. Give some account of Washington's retreat.

14. Why was the possession of the Hudson important?

15. How did the English plan to get possession of it?

16. What successes did Burgoyne meet?

17. What was the plan of St. Leger's expedition and who were with him?

18. Describe the battle of Oriskany.

19. Why was the defeat of St. Leger's troops especially important?

20. How was the march of Burgoyne hindered?

21. In what battles was he defeated?

22. Who was in command of the American army?

23. What were some of the effects of this victory?

24. How were the tories of the State treated?

25. In what year was the first State constitution adopted?

26. Give some of its provisions.

27. Who was the first governor of the State?

28. What did the English force in New York city do during the last years of the war?

29. What kept them from making further incursions into the State?

30. In what two ways did New York suffer?

31. Describe the massacre of Cherry Valley and other raids of the Indians and tories.

32. Give an account of Sullivan's expedition.

33. Why was this undertaken and with what result?

34. What other places suffered from the Indians?

35. Tell something about the capture of Stony Point.

36. What events happened at West Point, Tarrytown and Tappan?

37. Compare the treatment of Nathan Hale and that of Major Andre.

38. How did the English treat their prisoners?

39. Describe the last campaign of the war.

CHAPTER XI.

1. In what year were the Articles of Confederation adopted?

2. How many States had ratified them?

3. State their chief provisions.

4. Name some powers, now belonging to the United States government, which were then held by the legislature of the State.

5. What was the extent of the United States at the close of the Revolution?

6. What trouble arose over the land west of New York? How was this settled?

7. What position did the State take with regard to revenue taxes?

8. Why is the 25th of November celebrated in New York city?

9. Describe some of the changes which took place in the city during the war.

10. How were the tories treated?

11. How did the English break the treaty?

12. Name some causes which contributed to the growth of Albany.

13. How did Albany rank among the cities of the United States?

14. What part had the Iroquois taken in the war?

15. What was the result of this?

16. What was one way in which soldiers were rewarded for their services?

17. By whom was the central part of the State largely settled?

18. What was the population of the State?

19. How did it compare with that of 1880?

20. What was the population of New York city?

21. What legislative bodies met in that city?

22. Who was governor during these years?

23. For what purpose was the Board of Regents created?

24. Name some of the causes of the weakness of the Confederacy.

25. Did the action of New York tend to strengthen the Confederacy?

26. What was the object of the convention which met at Philadelphia in 1787?

27. Were the people of New York generally in favor of a new constitution?

28. How many of the delegates of the State remained through the convention?

29. What two parties grew up at this time?

30. Name some of the leading men of each.

31. What were the arguments used on each side?

32. What finally led New York to adopt the constitution?

33. How large was the majority in the convention favoring its adoption?

34. Why did not New York take part in the first presidential election?

35. Who were the first United States senators from the State?

36. When and where was Washington inaugurated?

PERIOD IV.

CHAPTER XII.

1. How long did congress meet in New York city and why was it removed?

2. What were the two parties?

3. What was the chief issue between them?

4. To which party did Governor Clinton belong?

5. Describe the State election of 1792.

6. Who was chosen governor at the next election?

7. Tell what you can about the Jay treaty.

8. How long was the governor's term of office?

9. How were the presidential electors chosen?

10. Describe the difficulty with Vermont.

11. How were the public lands disposed of ?

12. Mention some counties formed after the war.

13. How many counties were there in 1800?

14. What parts of the State were first settled and why?

15. In what ratio did the population increase from 1790 to 1800?

16. What plans were made for facilitating travel by water?

17. In what condition were most of the roads?

18. Tell about the newspapers published in the State.

19. Tell what you can of the mails and letters.

20. Describe the appearance of New York city at this time and tell how it was supplied with water.

21. Name two towns which were springing up on the Hudson.

22. When and where was the capital permanently located?

23. What rank did New York have with the other States in 1800?

24. What was the chief occupation of the people?

25. What other industries were being developed?

26. What was the first college organized by the Regents?

27. When was State money first given to the common schools?

28. How many slaves were there in New York?

29. What governor did much to abolish slavery?

30. What was the Council of Appointment? Of Revision?

31. Describe Jay's difficulty with these councils and how it was settled.

32. What war was threatening at this time?

33. Who was chosen governor in 1801?

CHAPTER XIII.

1. Who introduced the spoils system in this State?

2. What is meant by this system?

3. Name the most influential republicans at this time?
4. How was Burr regarded and why?
5. Tell something of Livingston.
6. Who was the leader in the State during the first twenty-five years of the 19th century?
7. Tell something of his early public life.
8. Describe the duel between Hamilton and Burr.
9. What were some of its results?
10. Briefly describe Burr's after life.
11. What was the beginning of the permanent school fund?
12. How had money been raised for school purposes before?
13. Were all the schools free at this time?
14. Mention some of the events of the year 1807 that show progress.
15. Tell something of Noah Webster.
16. Who was the first master of American literature, and what were some of his works?
17. What progress had manufacturers made?
18. Describe the first trip of the Clermont.
19. What two European countries were at war at this time, and how did this affect the United States?
20. What is an embargo?
21. Why did the embargo affect New York more than other States?
22. What changes were made in president and governor during the years 1808 and 1809?
23. Was the embargo a success?
24. Were the people of the State generally in favor of the war of 1812?
25. What acts of England led to a change of feeling?
26. Compare the condition of the State in the war of 1812 and of the Revolution.
27. What part of the State suffered most?
28. Describe the two lines of defences along the Niagara river.
29. What victories did the Americans gain in Canada?
30. What villages were burned by the English?
31. What victories freed western New York from danger?
32. Describe the campaign along Lake Ontario and the St. Lawrence.
33. Was the greater part of the war fought on land or sea?
34. What made New York city an important point?
35. Describe the preparations made.

36. Describe the expedition of the English to Lake Champlain and the battles fought.

37. What was gained by the war?

38. Who was the first Superintendent of Schools?

39. What military academy was organized at the beginning of this war?

40. Tell what you can about the Sunday schools of New York.

CHAPTER XIV.

1. On what were the parties of the State divided after the war of 1812?

2. Who headed the opposition to Clinton?

3. Through whose influence had Governor Tompkins received his first offices?

4. Tell something of the society of Tammany.

5. What names were given to the two factions of the democratic party?

6. To which did the Tammany men belong?

7. What State was a rival of New York?

8. Who succeeded Madison as president?

9. Why did the people of New York think that the president should come from the north?

10. What compromise was made?

11. How long was Tompkins governor of the State?

12. What was one of his last and most illustrious acts?

13. What former governor had labored to free the slaves and with what effect?

14. Give the date of their final emancipation.

15. For what is July 4, 1817, notable?

16. Name the natural water routes of the State.

17. Give the early history of the canal.

18. What route was suggested by Washington?

19. Why was the route through New York preferable?

20. Who was the first man to put these projects in definite shape, and what did he advise?

21. To whose efforts is the canal due?

22. Who surveyed the route?

23. Name some of the committee appointed to go over the route.

24. To what lake did they first plan the canal?

25. What was the estimated cost of a canal to Lake Erie?

26. Why did New York ask congress to build the canal and with what result?

27. Why was Clinton not a candidate for governor in 1822?
28. Tell what you can of the removal of Gideon Hawley.
29. What was the Albany Regency?
30. How many national parties were there at this time?
31 What party was growing up in New York?
32. What two reforms did its leaders advocate?
33. What bill was carried through the legislature by the enemies of Clinton?
34. What action did the people's party take?
35. Why was Clinton's election particularly fitting at this time?
36. What was the first cost of the canal?
37. The entire cost?
38. Give its dimensions and describe its course.
39. How is the water furnished, and in which direction does it flow?
40. When was the water first let in?
41. How was this fact made known in New York city?
42. What events during the war of 1812 made the necessity of a canal more apparent?
43. What were some of the objections made to the plan?
44. In what year was the work begun?
45. Between what two cities was the canal first made?
46. How was opposition to the scheme shown in 1819, and with what result?
47. How long was the first constitution in force?
48. Name some members of the constitutional convention of 1821.
49. In what year was the second constitution adopted?
50. What change was made in regard to property qualification of voters?
51. What councils were abolished and to whom were their powers given?
52. What courts were established?
53. At what number were the senate and assembly fixed?
54. How was the governor's term changed?
55. Who succeeded Clinton as governor?
56. Describe the first trip to the ocean.
57. Give an account of the celebration in New York city.
58. What progress had the State made in 1825?

PERIOD V.

CHAPTER XV.

1. Mention some changes which took place in the next twenty years.

2. To what did Clinton turn his attention after the completion of the Erie canal?

3. Describe his death and character.

4. Who was the leading man of the State after his death?

5. What change was made in 1828 in the manner of chosing presidential electors?

6. To what office had Van Buren been elected and why did he leave it?

7. Give a description of the rise of the anti-masons.

8. How strong did the anti-masonic party become?

9. Who was elected governor in 1832?

10. What name did the opponents of the democratic party take?

11. Who was their first candidate for governor?

12. Who was the first president from New York?

13. Tell something of the prosperity of these times.

14. Describe the panic of 1837.

15. How did this affect the election of 1838?

16. What led to the anti-rent troubles?

17. Describe the anti-rent rebellion.

18. How were the difficulties settled?

19. Tell something of the Patriot war.

20. What plans were made for opening up the southern counties?

21. When and where was the first railroad of the State built?

22. What canals were built?

23. Tell something of the travel on these canals. What was their chief use?

24. Tell of the decrease in the cost of freight.

25. What was the population of the State in 1850?

26. Tell what you can of the growth of New York city?

27. What change was made in lighting the city?

28. What took the place of the stages?

29. When and by whom was the telegraph invented?

30. State what you can of the newspapers of this period.

31. Name some of the prominent business men.

32. Tell something of the riots. What has made the city more orderly?

33. What disasters were supposed to be the result of the insufficient supply of water?

34. Describe the first Croton aqueduct.

35. Tell what you can of Central Park.

36. Name some of the distinguished people who were publicly welcomed in New York city.

CHAPTER XVI.

1. Tell something of the early history of education in the State.
2. What governors and what secretary of state were especially interested in schools?
3. What means were taken to provide qualified teachers?
4. What were the county superintendents?
5. Where was the first normal school?
6. How were the expenses of the common schools paid?
7. What were the principal changes made by the third constitution?
8. Give an account of the passage and repeal of the free school act.
9. What school office was created in 1854?
10. What changes has invention made in the daily life of the people?
11. What improvements were made in morals?
12. What connection with the history of New York have the Shakers, Mormons, Millerites, John H. Noyes, and John Brown?

CHAPTER XVII.

1. What stand was taken by the people of the State in regard to slavery in the early part of the century?
2. Give an account of the trouble between Virginia and New York.
3. How were the admission of Texas, the Mexican war, and the compromise of 1850 regarded?
4. What party sprang up and for what purpose?
5. Who was the first republican governor?
6. Who was the candidate for president from New York at the republican national convention of 1860?
7. What office did he hold during the war?
8. Were all the people of the State united in favoring the war?
9. What was the position of New York city?
10. How did New York respond to Lincoln's first call?
11. How were the people affected by the battle of Bull Run?
12. How many soldiers did New York send during the first year of the war?
13. In what other ways did the State aid the union?
14. Who was elected governor in 1862? Of what party was he?
15. Give an account of the Draft Riots.
16. How many troops did New York furnish during the war?
17. What is the 15th amendment to the constitution?

18. In what year did New York ratify it?
19. In what year were the schools of the State made free?
20. How was the number of academies and academic departments increased?

CHAPTER XVIII.

1. Tell what you can of the political history of the State since 1870.

.2. What change was made in the term of office of the governor in 1876?

3. Who was elected to that position in 1882? Who succeeded him as governor?

4. What candidates for president and vice-president have come from this State?

5. Which of these have been elected?

6. What was the Tweed Ring?

7. By what paper was it exposed, and what was the result of the exposure?

8. What was the population of New York city in 1880?

9. In what two ways was rapid transit obtained in the city?

10. Tell what you can of the Statue of Liberty and of the capitol at Albany.

11. Mention places in the State noted for beautiful scenery and as summer resorts.

12. What was the population of the State in 1880?

13. In what respects was it first?

14. Compare its foreign and domestic traffic with that of other States.

15. What can you say of it as an agricultural State? Name some of its products.

16. Tell something of its manufacturing interests.

17. Give an account of its schools.

18. What centennial celebrations have been held in New York?

INDEX.

Abercrombie, Gen., 72, 73
Adams, John, 119, 120, 125, 148
Adams, John Quincy, 149
Albany (city) 16, 35, 37, 43, 62, 70, 80, 101, 112, 122, 123, 145
Albany (county) 80
Allen, Ethan, 97, 98
Andre, Major, 107, 108
Andros, Edmund, 39, 40, 42, 43, 45, 46
Anti-federalists, 115, 116, see republicans, 119
Anti-masons, 150
Anti-Rent Rebellion, 152, 153
Aqueduct, Croton, 157, 158
Arnold, Benedict, 99, 102, 107, 108
Arthur, Chester A., 173
Assembly (colonial), 43, 56, 58, 60, 63, 65, 68
Astor, John Jacob, 156

Battery, the, 47
Beecher, Henry Ward, 164
Bellomont, Gov., 56
Bennett, James Gordon, 156
Benson, Egbert, 116
Black Rock, 132, 133
Block, Adrian, 14
Bogardus, Everardus, 31
Bouck, William C., 153, 162
Bradford, William, 64
Brant, Joseph, 101, 106
Brooklyn, 15, 19, 41, 75
Brown, John, 164
Bryant, William Cullen, 156
Buchanan, James, 166, 167
Bucktails, 137
Buffalo, 113, 122, 132, 133, 145, 151
Burgoyne, Gen., 101, 102, 103
Burnet, Gov., 62, 63
Burr, Aaron, 119, 126, 127, 128, 161
Butler, Walter, 105, 106

Cabot, 9, 13
Canada, 10, 49-54, 98, 99, 101, 153, 154
Canals, 121, 139, 148, 154, 155, see Erie canal.
Capitol, 175
Castle Island, 13, 16
Centennial Celebrations, 178
Central Park, 158
Champlain, Samuel, 9, 10, 11, 12
Chapin, E. H., 164
Cherry Valley, 105
Civil war, 164, 169
Clark, Myron H., 162
Clarke, George, 65, 66, 67
Clermont, 129, 130
Cleveland, Grover, 172, 173
Clinton, Admiral, 67, 69
Clinton, Dewitt, 113, 114, 115, 131, 132, 137, 138, 140, 141, 143-146, 148, 149, 154, 159, 161
Clinton, Gen. (English), 103, 107, 108
Clinton, George, 89, 98, 104, 113, 114, 119, 125-127, 131, 139
Clinton, James, 105
Clintonians, 137
Colden, Cadwallader, 82, 87, 93, 139
Columbia College, 78, 113, 135
Columbus, 9
Colve, Anthony, 38, 39
Commerce. See trade.
Confederation, Articles of, 109, 111
Congress, Colonial, 86
Congress, Continental, 91, 98, 100, 109, 110, 113, 114
Conkling, Roscoe, 173
Connecticut, 22, 36, 40, 75, 90, 112
Constitutions, 103, 104, 111-116, 141, 142, 160
Cooper, Fenimore, 107
Cooper, Peter, 156
Cornbury, Lord, 57, 58, 60
Cornell, Alonzo B., 172
Cornell University, 170

Cornwallis, Gen.,   108
Cosby, Gov.,   63-65
Council (colonial),   56
Council of appointment,   124, 142
Council of revision,   125, 142
Counties,   45, 75, 79, 80, 120, 121, 146, 163
Criminals,   18, 129
Crown Point,   71, 73, 98
Customs,   30, 32, 42, 81, 82, 163

De Lancy, Stephen,   63, 70
Delaware. State of,   36
Democrats,   143, 151, 168
Dunmore, Gov.,   92
Dickens, Charles,   158
Dickinson, Daniel S.,   163
Dix, John A.,   159, 172
Dongan Charter,   43, 44, 45
Dongan, Thomas,   43, 45, 52
Draft Riots,   168, 169
Draper, Andrew S.,   177
Dress,   31, 81, 82
Duke of York,   34, 39, 44, 45, 46
Duke's Laws, the   36

Education, see schools.
Edward, Fort,   71, 72, 101
Embargo,   130, 131
Erie Canal,   11, 130, 139-146, 155
Esopus,   19, 24, 37, 43
Evacuation Day,   110
Evarts, William M.,   173
Evertsen, Cornelis,   38

Falls, Niagara,   175
Federalists,   115,
            118, 119, 120, 125, 126, 131, 132, 137
Fenton, Reuben E.,   169, 170
Field, Cyrus W.,   156
Fish, Hamilton,   162, 163
Fitch, John,   122, 130
Fletcher, Gov.,   55, 56, 64
France,   9, 103, 125
Franklin, Benjamin,   70
Fremont, John C.,   166

French,   10, 11, 15, 47-55, 61, 69-73, 108
Frontenac, Count,   52, 53
Frontenac, Fort,   51, 52, 62, 71, 73
Fulton, Robert,   129, 140

Gates, Gen.,   103
Geddes, Joseph,   140
Genet,   125
German Flats,   61, 105
Grant, Gen.,   170, 173
Greeley, Horace,   156, 166, 173
Greenback Party,   173

Half Moon, the,   12, 13
Hale, Nathan,   107, 108
Hamilton, Alexander,   79, 93, 112,
                    114, 115, 118, 125, 127, 128
Hamilton, Andrew,   64, 65
Hamilton College,   123, 135
Harrison, William Henry,   152
Hawley, Gideon,   143
Hendrick, King,   70
Herkimer, Gen.,   101, 102
Hill, David B.,   172
Hoffman, John T.,   170, 172
Houses,   29
Howe, Gen.,   99, 100
Hudson, Henry,   9, 10, 11, 12, 13
Hudson, river,   10, 11, 14, 51, 101, 107, 108, 123
Hudson (city),   123
Hunt, Washington,   162
Hunter, Robert,   60, 61, 62

Ingoldsby, Richard,   47
Irondequoit Bay,   52
Iroquois,   9, 10, 11, 17, 18, 19, 37, 49-54, 70, 72,
      83, 89, 98, 101, 102, 104, 106, 110, 112, 133, 139
Irving, Washington,   17, 129, 158

Jackson, Gen.,   149, 151
James II., see Duke of York.
Jay, John.
      91, 98, 104, 115, 118, 119, 124-126, 138, 148
Jay, Peter,   139

Jay, William, 139
Jefferson, Thomas,
　　　118, 119, 125,126, 127, 131, 148
Jesuits, 49-51
Jogues, Isaac, 49
Johnson, John, 98, 101, 106
Johnson, Sir William, 70 73, 83, 89, 94

Kent, James, 142
Kidd, Captain, 56
Kieft, William 17-19, 21, 21, 27
King, John A. 162, 166
King, Rufus, 116, 118, 112
King's College, see Columbia.
Kingston, 80, 103, 107
Kirkland, Samuel, 123
Kossuth, 158

Labor Parties, 173
Lafayette, 58
Lamb, John, 91, 93
Le Moyne, 50
Lansing, 114, 115
Lee, Ann, 164
Lee, Gen., 108
Leisler, Jacob, 46-48
Leislerians, 55
Lewis, Morgan, 127, 128, 131
Lincoln, Abraham, 166, 167, 169
Lind, Jenny, 158
Livingston, Brockholst, 120, 127
Livingston, Robert, 59, 60, 98
Livingston, Robert R.,
　　　115, 116, 126, 129, 140, 149
Long Island,
　　9, 11, 15, 22, 37, 41, 43, 60, 61, 75, 100
Lovelace, Lord, 37, 38
Lundy's Lane, 133

Mac donough, Commodore, 134, 135
Madison, President, 131, 132, 138
Mails, 81, 122
Manhattan Island, 13, 18, 19
Manning, Captain, 38
Manufactures, 123, 129, 176, 177

Marcy, William L., 143, 151, 163
Martha's Vineyard, 36, 40
May, Captain, 14, 16
McClellan, Gen., 168
McDougal, Alexander, 91, 93
Megapolensis, John, 27
Mexican War, 165
Milborne, 47, 48
Miller, William, 164
Mining, 123
Minnet, Peter, 16-19, 21
Mohegans, 10
Money, 42, 60
Monroe, President, 138, 143, 118
Montcalm, 71, 72, 73
Montgomery, Richard, 98, 99
Montreal, 13, 52, 53
Morgan, Edwin D., 166
Morgan, William, 150
Morris, Gouverneur, 79, 126, 127, 139, 140
Morris, Lewis, 59, 60, 64
Morse, Samuel F. B., 156

Nantucket, 36
Navigation Laws 84
Negro Plot, 66, 67
New Amsterdam, 15, 20, 25, 28,
　　see New York City.
New France, 49, 51
New Netherland, 11, 19
Newspapers, 64, 84, 85, 122, 129, 156
New York city, 37, 51, 61, 66, 76 78, 82,
　　85-88, 91-93, 99, 100, 104, 111, 113, 116, 118,
　　122, 125, 129, 132, 134, 145, 146, 151, 155-158,
　　167-169, 174, see New Amsterdam.
Niagara, Fort, 52, 63, 69, 70, 73, 112, 132
Nichols, Richard, 31-37
Nicholson, 45, 46
Non-importation, 88, 89
Normal schools, 160, 170, 177
Noyes, John H., 164

Ogdensburg, 69, 74, 112, 133
Oriskany, battle, 101, 102
Orange, Fort, 16, 19, 35
Oswego, 62, 70, 71, 73, 80, 101, 102, 112, 133

Palmyra, 164
Panics, financial, 151, 173
Parties, 45, 119, 125, 137, 143, 166, 172, 173
Patriot war, 153, 154
Patroons, 16, 82
Pavonia, 15, 19, 22
Pemaquid, 43
Penn, William, 43
People's Party, 143, 144
Physicians, 129
Pirates, 55, 56
Pitt, 73, 88
Plattsburgh, 134
Population, 19, 20, 40, 61, 76,
112, 113, 121, 123, 146, 155, 169, 174, 175
Poughkeepsie, 80, 115, 175
Prisons, 128, 163
Produce, 41, 163, 176
Prohibition, 162, 173
Puritans, 34

Quakers, 20, 78, 139
Quartering Act, 85, 88
Quebec, 73, 90
Queen Anne's War, 53, 54
Queenstown Heights, 133

Railroads, 154
Randall, Samuel S., 160
Raymond, Henry J., 156
Regents, 113, 123, 170, 171
Religion, 31, 45, 49, 55, 77, 78, 91, 164
Rensselaerwick, 16, 19, 43
Republicans (democratic-republican party),
110, 125, 126, 127, see anti-federalists,
and democrats.
Republican party (modern), 166, 169
Rice, Victor M., 162
Roads, 122, 154
Robinson, Lucius, 172
Rochester, 144, 145, 151
Roelandsen, Adam, 32
Rome, 74, 139, 141

Sackett's Harbor, 133

Sandy Hook, 10, 13, 134
Saratoga, 69, 80, 108
Schenectady, 20, 27, 51, 52, 61, 80
Schools, 32, 41, 79, 123, 124, 128,
135, 136, 143, 148, 159-162, 170, 171, 177
Schuyler, Peter, 53, 55, 59, 63
Schuyler, Philip, 89, 98, 99,
101, 103, 112, 115, 116, 118, 119
Sears, Isaac, 88, 98
Seward, William H., 151, 153, 163, 165, 166
Seymour, Horatio, 162, 168, 170
Shakers, 160
Slaves, 20, 67, 124, 138, 163-174
Sloughter, Gov., 47, 48, 55
Smith, Joseph, 164
Smith, Melancthon, 115
Smith, William, 59, 60, 64, 65, 70
Sons of Liberty, 65, 85, 88, 91-94, 112
Spencer, Ambrose, 142
Stamp Act, 84, 85, 87, 88
Stanwix, Fort, 101, 102, 105
Steamboats, 129
Steuben, Gen., 112
Stewart, Alexander T., 156
St. Leger, Gen., 101-103
Stony Point, 107
Stuyvesant, Peter, 17, 21, 23-25, 27
Sullivan, Gen., 105, 106
Sunday Schools, 135, 136
Swedes, 21
Syracuse, 10, 151

Tammany, 137
Throop, Enos T., 149, 150
Ticonderoga, Fort, 71-73, 98, 101
Tilden, Samuel J., 172, 173
Tompkins, Daniel D., 131, 137, 138, 141, 142, 149
Tories, 45, 89, 93, 94, 103, 105, 111, 112
Trade, 17, 37, 42, 61, 63, 92, 112, 158, 176
Travel, 80, 156, 174
Troy, 123
Tryon, Gov., 92, 95
Tryon (county), 106
Tweed, William H., 174
Twelve Men, the, 24, 27

Underhill, John, 23

Union College, 123, 135
Ury, John. 67
Utica, 74, 141, 151, 165

Van Buren, Martin, 137, 142, 143, 149, 151, 152, 154
Van Curler, 27
Van Dam, Rip, 63, 64
Van Rensselaer, Kilian, 16
Van Rensselaer, Stephen, 2, 142
Van Twiller, Walter, 17
Vermont, 90, 97, 120
Virginia, 115, 138
Vries, de, 2

Warner, Seth, 97, 98
Washington, Fort, 100
Washington, Geo., 11, 98-100, 103-105, 108, 110, 111, 114, 116, 118, 119, 125, 130
Watervliet, 161
Wayne, Anthony, 107

Webster, Noah, 127
Weed, Thurlow, 156
West Indian Company, Dutch, 10
West Point, 107
Wheeler, William A., 177
Whigs, 151, 152, 166
White, Hugh, 113
Whitestown, 113, 122
Wilkinson, Jemima, 164
William Henry, Fort, 71, 72
William, King, 46
Wolfe, Gen., 73
Wright, Silas, 153, 162, 163

Yates, 114, 115
Yates, Joseph C., 134
Yorktown, 108
Young, John, 153, 162

Zenger, Peter, 64, 65

GOVERNORS OF NEW YORK.

COLONIAL.

Cornelius Jacobsen May, 1621
William Verhulst, 1625
Peter Minuet. 1626
Wouter Van Twiller, 1633
William Kieft, 1638
Peter Stuyvesant, 1647
Richard Nicolls, 1664
Francis Lovelace, 1668
Cornelis Evertse, Jr.,* 1673
Anthony Colve, 1673
Edmund Andros, 1674
Anthony Brockholles,† 1677
Sir Edmund Andros, Knt.,1678
Anthony Brockholles,† 1681
Thomas Dongan, 1683
Sir Edmund Andros, 1688
Francis Nicholson,‡ 1688
Jacob Leisler, 1689
Henry Sloughter, 1691.
Richard Ingoldesby,† 1691
Benjamin Fletcher, 1692

Earl of Bellamont, 1698
John Nanfan,‡ 1699
Earl of Bellamont, 1700
Eldest Councillor present.§ 1701
John Nanfan,‡ 1701
Lord Cornbury, 1702
Lord Lovelace, 1708
Peter Schuyler.§ 1709
Richard Ingoldesby,‡ 1709
Peter Schuyler,§ 1709
Richard Ingoldesby,‡ 1709
Gerardus Beeckman,§ 1710
Robert Hunter, 1710
Peter Schuyler,§ 1719
William Burnet, 1720
John Montgomery, 1728
Rip Van Dam,§ 1731
William Cosby, 1732
George Clarke,§ 1736
George Clarke,‡ 1736

George Clinton, 1743
Sir Danvers Osborne, Bart., 1753
James De Lancey,‡ 1753
Sir Charles Hardy, Kut., 1755
James De Lancey,‡ 1757
Cadwallader Colden,§ 1760
Cadwallader Colden,‡ 1761
Robert Monckton, 1761
Cadwallader Colden,‡ 1761
Robert Monckton, 1762
Cadwallader Colden,‡ 1763
Sir Henry Moore, Bart., 1765
Cadwallader Colden,‡ 1769
Earl of Dunmore, 1770
William Tryon, 1771
Cadwallader Colden,‡ 1771
William Tryon, 1775
James Robertson, 1780
Andrew Elliott,‡ ‖ 1783

* And a Council of War.   ‡ Lieutenant-Governor.
† Commander-in-Chief.   § President of the Council.
‖ Military Governors during the Revolution. not recognized by the State of New York.

PRESIDENTS OF THE PROVINCIAL CONGRESS, Etc.

Peter van Brugh Livingston, 1775
Nathaniel Woodhull,* 1775
Abraham Yates, Jr.,* 1775
* Pro-tempore.

Nathaniel Woodhull. 1775
John Haring,* 1776
Abraham Yates, Jr.,* 1776
Abraham Yates, Jr., 1776

Peter R. Livingston, 1776
Abraham Ten Broeck, 1777
Leonard Gansevoort,* 1777
Pierre Van Cortlandt,† 1777
† President of the Council of Safety.

GOVERNORS SINCE ADOPTION OF THE CONSTITUTION.

George Clinton, 1777
John Jay, 1795
George Clinton, 1801
Morgan Lewis. 1804
Daniel D. Tompkins. 1807
John Tayler,* 1817
DeWitt Clinton. 1817
Joseph C. Yates, 1823
DeWitt Clinton, 1825
Nathaniel Pitcher.* 1828
Martin Van Buren, 1829
Enos T. Throop.* 1829

Enos T. Throop, 1831.
William L. Marcy, 1833
William H. Seward, 1839
William C. Bouck, 1843
Silas Wright, 1845
John Young, 1847
Hamilton Fish, 1849
Washington Hunt, 1851
Horatio Seymour. 1853
Myron H. Clark, 1855
John . King. 1857
Edwin D. Morgan, 1859

Horatio Seymour, 1863
Reuben E. Fenton, 1865
John T. Hoffman, 1869
John A. Dix, 1873
Samuel J. Tilden, 1875
Lucius Robinson, 1877
Alonzo B. Cornell, 1880
Grover Cleveland, 1883
David B. Hill,* 1885
David B. Hill, 1886
Roswell P. Flower, 1892

* Lieutenant-Governor acting as Governor.

(204)

BOOKS ON NEW YORK STATE HISTORY.

Without attempting to give a bibliography of New York State history, a classified list of the most helpful books is appended.

STATE HISTORIES.

New York, American Commonwealth Series, 2 vols. (to 1885), Ellis H. Roberts.

Empire State (to 1887), Benson ... Lossing.

History of the State of New York, 2 vols. (to 1691), John R. Broadhead.

History of New York, 2 vols. (to 1789), William Dunlap.

Documentary History of New York, 4 vols., E. B. O'Callaghan.

History of the Province of New York (to 1762) William Smith. (See p. 59, note, *supra*).

Political History of New York, 2 vols. (1788–1841), Jabez D. Hammond.

History of Political Parties in the State of New York (1783-1844), J. S. Jenkins.

The Natural, Statistical and Civil History of the State of New York, 3 vols. (to 1800), James Macauley.

History of New Netherland, E. B. O'Callaghan.

New York during the Revolutionary War, 2 vols., Thomas Jones.

History of New York State (to 1870), S. S. Randall.

NEW YORK CITY.

History of the City of New York, 2 vols. (to 1878), Mrs. Martha J. Lamb.

Shorter works under similar titles by Mary L. Booth (to 1859), William L. Stone (to 1870), D. T. Valentine (to 1853), and Benson J. Lossing.

New York, Historic Towns Series, Theodore Roosevelt.

Story of the City of New York, Charles Burr Todd.

Memorial History of the City of New York (to be completed in four volumes to 1892) Gen. J. G. Wilson.

INDIANS AND FRENCH IN NEW YORK.

History of the Five Nations, Cadwallader Colden.

Notes on the Iroquois, Henry Rowe Schoolcraft.

League of the Iroquois, Lewis Henry Morgan.

Parkman's Works, especially, Pioneers of France in the New World, The Jesuits in North America, The Old Regime in Canada, Count Frontenac and New France under Louis XIV., Montcalm and Wolfe.

BIOGRAPHIES.

The following biographies are in the American Statesmen Series :

Alexander Hamilton, Henry Cabot Lodge.

Gouverneur Morris, Theodore Roosevelt.

Martin Van Buren, Edward M. Shepard.

John Jay, George Pellew.

In the Makers of America Series, Sir William Johnson and the Six Nations, William Elliot Griffis, is a recent and valuable contribution to New York history.

Biographies of Johnson, Brant and Red Jacket, William L. Stone.

Lives of the Governors of New York, 1 vol. (to 1850), J. S. Jenkins.

Life and Times of Philip Schuyler, 2 vols., Benson J. Lossing.

J. Fenimore Cooper, American Men of Letters Series, Thomas R. Lounsbury.

This list might be extended. In th libraries furnished the school districts of the State some years ago are short biographies of some of the leading men of the State.

FICTION.

Cooper's Novels, especially The Spy, Satanstoe, Miles Wallingford and the Leather: stocking Tales.

Story of a New York House, H. C. Bunner. (New York city in the early part of the XIX Century.)

In the Valley, Harold Frederic. (Mohawk valley in Revolutionary times.)

In Leisler's Times, Elbridge S. Brooks.

The Begum's Daughter. Edwin Lassetter Bynner. (Colonial).

The Bow of Orange Ribbon, Amelia E. Barr. (Revolution).

The Dutchman's Fireside, James Kirke Paulding.

MISCELLANEOUS.

The Magazine of American History.

Travels in New England and New York (1821-22), Theodore Dwight.

Narrative and Critical History of the United States (under Middle Colonies in vol. V. and the English in New York in vol. III.), Winsor.

Centennial Celebrations of the State of New York, issued by the Regents of the University.

General Sullivan's Indian Expedition, issued by the Secretary of State.

Journal of a Voyage to New York in 1679-80, Jason Dankers and Peter Sluyler.

Knickerbocker History of New York, Washington Irving.

Frontiersmen of New York, Jeptha R. Simms.

Journal of a Tour to Niagara Falls in 1805, Timothy Bigelow.

The Story of New York State, Elbridge S. Brooks.

LOCAL HISTORIES.

Sections of the State are treated in such works as Reminiscences of Western New York, J. L. Barton, Annals of Tryon County, William W. Campbell, and History of Long Island Thompson.

Each county and many of the towns and cities have their published histories. It is unnecessary to enumerate.

NOTE.—In answer to teachers who have asked for hints in extending the ten or fifteen weeks' work in this volume to twenty weeks, the author has these suggestions to make :

With some of the books above noted the history of New York may be further pursued topically. Such subjects as Dutch customs and manners, the French in New York, boundary disputes with Connecticut, Massachusetts, New Hampshire, Pennsylvania, New Jersey and New France, the constitutions of New York, the Iroquois confederacy, the Erie canal, the anti-masonic movement, the anti-rent rebellion, the school history of New York, the statesmen, inventors, men of letters and business men of New York, and like topics, suggest fields for reading and investigation.

Another line of work that will profitably fill two or three weeks of the term in this connection is the study of local history. Beside reading county and town histories of his section, the pupil should be directed to examine the files of local papers and to obtain facts and incidents from old residents : if then with these data he writes a history of his town or county he will get an idea of the sources of history and come to a better understanding of what history is.

Waterfalls

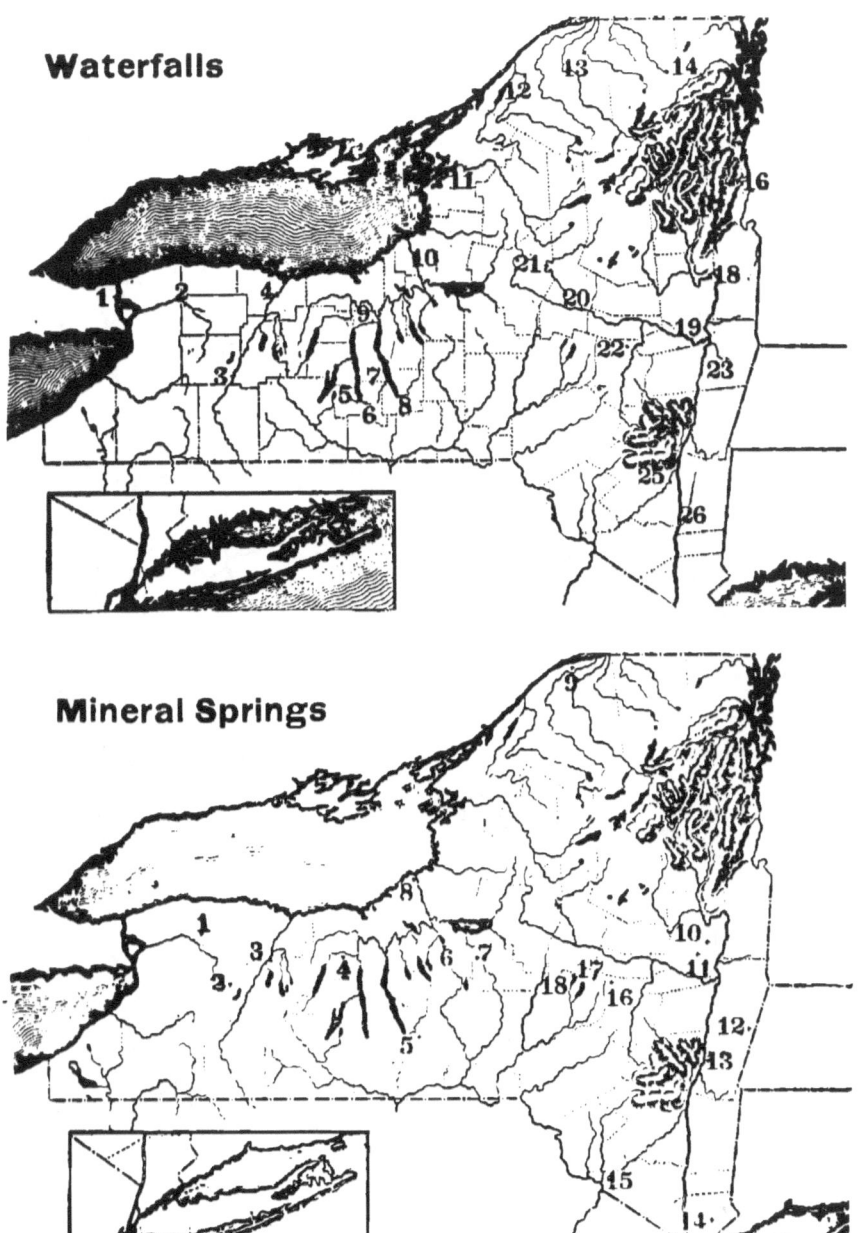

Mineral Springs

Colleges

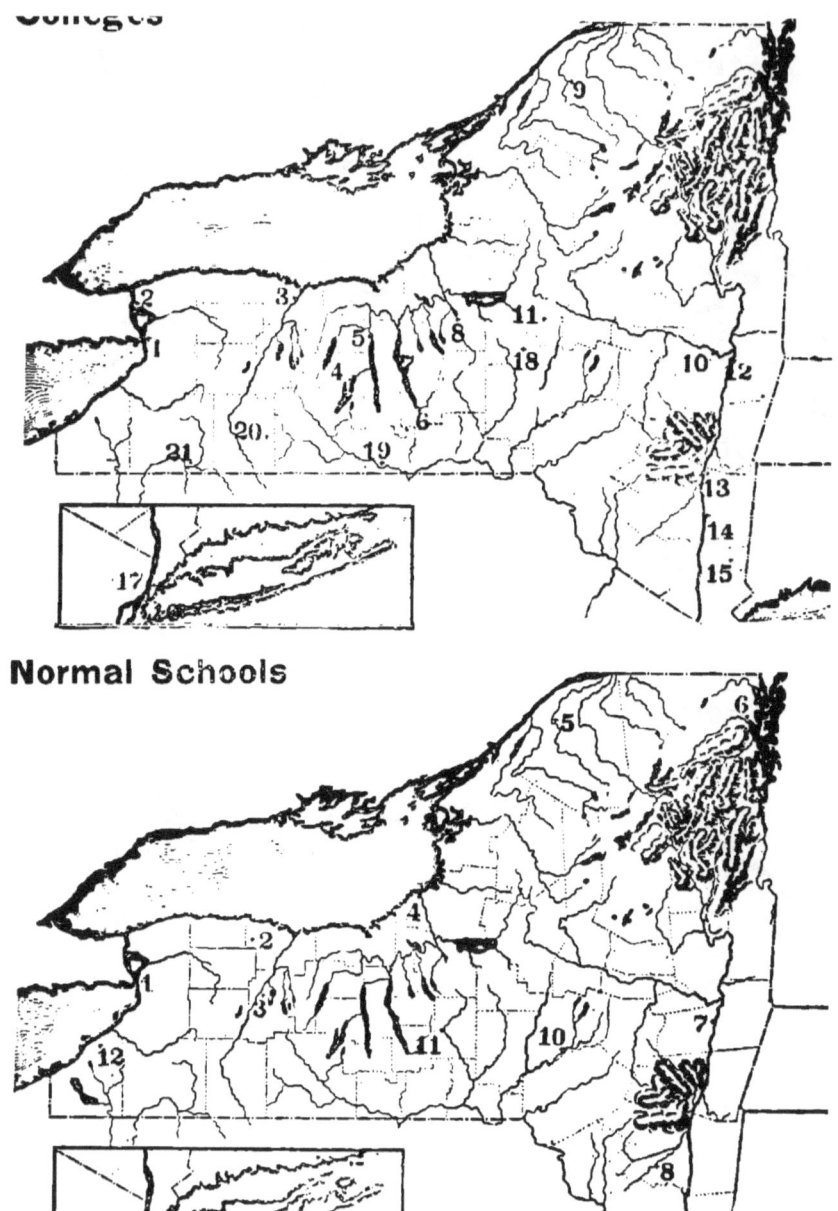

Normal Schools